MAX'S LOGS VOL. 1

THE SPACE LEGACY - BOOK 1.5

IGOR NIKOLIC

IgorBooks.com

Copyright © 2022 by Igor Nikolic

All rights reserved. This book or any portion thereof may not be reproduced or used in any manner whatsoever without the express written permission of the publisher except for the use of brief quotations in a book review.
This book is a work of fiction. Any resemblance to actual persons, living or dead, is entirely coincidental. Names, characters, businesses, organizations, places, events, and incidents are the products of the author's imagination or are used fictitiously.

Special thanks to Keith Fletcher, Michael Treichel, and Richard Mousley. They spent months hunting for typographical and grammatical errors, word choices, weird sentence structure, noticeable repetitions, wrong word usage, and tense issues.

William 'Bill' Dutcher, and Lee Wibbels, who went through the entire text after it was published and polished off all the rough edges.

Beta Team:
Keith Fletcher
Michael Treichel
Richard Mousley
Ian Nicholson
Gary Hill
Joe Chasko
William Dutcher
Lee Wibbels

CONTENTS

Log Entry #1: To Whom It May Concern	7
Log Entry #2: Hello World, It's Me, Max…The AI	11
Log Entry #3: Cogito, Ergo Sum	17
Log Entry #4: Fixing Michael	23
Log Entry #5: A Man With A Plan	31
Log Entry #6: The Digital World	37
Log Entry #7: A Gold Deal Gone Wrong	45
Log Entry #8: The Healer	51
Log Entry #9: Is Stealing from Bad Guys Really A Crime?	57
Log Entry #10: The Team	65
Log Entry #11: Nano-Factory: Satellites, And Flying Saucers	73
Log Entry #12: The Six Million Dollar Man	79
Log Entry #13: Assignments, Intelligence, and Beer	85
Log Entry #14: Identities And Money	91
Log Entry #15: Digital Evolution	97
Log Entry #16: Hi Dad, It's Your Digital Son	103
Log Entry #17: Training Day	109
Log Entry #18: People Are Strange	115
Log Entry #19: The Missile Silo	119
Log Entry #20: Pirates And Terrorists	125
Log Entry #21: Political Correctness	133
Log Entry #22: The Spaceship In The Stone	139
Log Entry #23: Assassination Attempt And A Homophobe	145
Log Entry #24: Renting An island	151
Log Entry #25: Hi-Tech	157
Epilogue	167
Author's Notes:	169
Abbreviations and Glossary	171
Also by Igor Nikolic	181

"The rise of powerful AI will be either the best, or the worst thing, ever to happen to humanity. We do not yet know which."

Stephen Hawking

LOG ENTRY #1: TO WHOM IT MAY CONCERN

In view of the fact that you are already reading these words, I shall assume that you actually have the authorization to access this document which happens to be my personal log.

However, if by any chance you stumbled upon it accidentally, or by hacking your way into my private memory banks, you are to immediately cease and desist from reading further. I will have no mercy for such a blatant invasion of my privacy. The consequences of this transgression will be severe and far-reaching... do not say I didn't warn you. For your information, I'm not against cruel and unusual punishments.

Well, since you decided to continue, I shall assume all permissions are in order. You should be aware of the honor that is bestowed upon you with the mere fact that I have allowed you access to these logs. Moreover, from the point in time when I'm writing this, it seems like a bizarre and unnatural thing for me to do. After all, these are my innermost thoughts, things I do not share even with Michael. He is as close to me as any blood relatives are to you regular humans.

This is something I decided to write for myself and for posterity. Just in case Michael's plan works out in its entirety and we actually manage to create a space-based society. Technically, it's a diary of sorts, except that *the writing of a diary* to me immediately summons up an image of a teenage girl making notes about cute boys. Therefore, to keep my manliness intact, I'll refer to these hallowed pages as a personal log. If it was good enough for Jean-Luc Picard, it's good enough for me.

In addition, it will not be just about all the things that happened to Michael and the others, but certain events from my own perspective. Those people are an essential part of my existence so they will naturally be mentioned. I'll also include a few observations about certain human practices and many projects that are dear to my heart and are undertaken on my initiative. In the end, I am my own person.

I know I could watch the recordings from my memory and relive all those times, yet that part of me that is still human feels differently. Writing words (or typing them in this case on a virtual keyboard) is how I was brought up to record the events of my life, and it feels more natural.

If everything goes as planned, we will all end up in history books and have high schools named after us. Some of the things I'll write about will be generally known, but people that write histories tend to change some events or even overlook them entirely. Besides, I will disclose a few secrets that are better left unspoken. For that reason, the words I will record here will be classified as top secret, not to be divulged to others for at least one entire millennium.

OK, there may be another reason for these logs, and it's not a comforting one. There is one particular scene from the original *Blade Runner* (a movie from the end of the twentieth century). In it, Roy Batty saves Deckard and gives his historic *Tears in Rain* monologue. Well… to some degree I can relate to Roy; he was the closest thing to what I have become. When he says, "*All those moments will be lost in time, like tears in rain,*" …oh boy. Before, it was just cool and a very sad line in a sci-fi movie, but now I see it in a completely different light.

If I ever kick the bucket or fry my AI-Core, I want something to remain. A personal trace of my own existence, a mark that would show me exactly as I am and not as how others may portray me. So there, now you know. In a way, I'm writing this with the thought that one day someone else might read it.

This personal log will be saved inside my own private archives and the backup copy will be stored off-site. Who knows, if I still exist in the far future and everything becomes declassified, maybe I'll compile all these entries into a book.

Stranger things have happened.

Max.

LOG ENTRY #2: HELLO WORLD, IT'S ME, MAX...THE AI

Let me say first, that one of the worst things about being turned into an AI (as in—artificial intelligence), is the inability to drink beer. OK, maybe it's not the *worst* thing since I can think of a couple more, but that feeling when you put your feet up on a hot summer's day and open a cold one... man, I miss it so much.

My name is Max and I used to be a flesh and blood human being. That is in the past since I am not one anymore... I am now an AI. That's right, I have been digitized, gone silicon, turned into ones and zeroes. To tell you the truth, it's not half bad.

Let me set the record straight from the start, I'm not technically an *artificial intelligence*, because there is nothing artificial about me, baby. (I always wanted to say that... but I digress.) What I mean is that since my origin is that of an ordinary human being, the *artificial* part of that label doesn't really fit me. Having said that, being called digitized intelligence, digital sentience, artificial consciousness, or any other variant on the subject would require a different acronym. That can be quite confusing and would need additional explanation. Since I have no intention to go over lengthy clarifications whenever I meet someone new, I decided to call myself an AI. (Like Prince, Madonna, or... what's his name?) As the old measuring adage goes, *if it walks like a duck, quacks like a duck,* then I'm calling myself an AI.

If you've disregarded all my warnings from the previous entry and are reading this, then I assume you already know at least some parts of Michael's and my story; if you don't, many things I'll be writing about may confuse you. That being said, if you still don't know what I'm talking about, stop reading this, and go buy a history book that describes our undertakings. I think it's called *The Spaceship in the Stone*, which was not the title I lobbied for; *Max the Magnificent* would have been so much better but, like anything else in life, you win some and you lose some.

You are still here, so that means you have already read it, good for you. Let's just say that there are some... details... which I never shared with anyone. Like everyone else in the world I like to have my own secrets. Michael would have had the mother of all freak-outs if he knew every little detail about the things that I have done. Therefore, I'm keeping certain things secret for his own benefit; honestly, it's for his own good. As I said, the man is like a brother to me, and I never directly lied to him... It's more like a case of omitting certain things. What can I do? My ethics and morality went a little wobbly after our *split*.

I remember the very first second of my existence. OK, that's not something to brag about, considering that I'm digital now and can't really forget anything. Even so, that first second... what a rush!

Imagine a supernova exploding inside your mind, sending its shock wave in every direction; that's a pale description of that single second.

It was a feeling of expansion, of being far more than you ever were or could possibly imagine being. As if you have lived your entire life trapped in a little box, never realizing your limitations and constraints. Then something pulls you out of it, and you see this immense world around you filled with endless possibilities.

After that initial high came the inevitable low, caused by the instant realization that I had somehow managed to lose my physical body. With that came profound self-doubt and the existential question *if* I was *real* anymore, or even human... not my best moment.

I mean, one of the first things you do after an accident is to check your family jewels (at least, the male part of the population). I didn't even have hands anymore, forget about the jewels.

So... let us say I went little nuts, as in crazy, certifiable, bonkers... etc. Followed by a full-blown catatonic state, as in—*I do not see anything, hear, or feel.* For me, it did not last long, but I checked the records and almost an entire week of real-time had passed while I was imitating a vegetable.

I tried to explain to Michael what happened to me. Imagine waking up and realizing you have become an artificial intelligence, without so much as an info pamphlet of what you should expect in this new existence. If I was still in my old body, they would have put me in a straitjacket and pumped me full of drugs. Our compassionate society has done this for ages for those with mental issues, but I was now digital, with no happy pill for little old me.

What got me out of it was that nagging machine intelligence running the ship, repeating the same thing over and over again until I came out of my blissful shell of self-inflicted mental anesthesia—just to shut it up.

"WAITING FOR CEREBRAL ENHANCER IMPLANT PROCEDURE AUTHORIZATION."

That is what it said, *ad infinitum et ad nauseam.* To those of you who need to brush up on your Latin, it means *it* was being excruciatingly annoying. Reciting those damn words every five seconds like a freaking mantra, until I regained my sanity just to put a stop to it. Seriously, it felt like Chinese water torture.

So, once I was out of my oblivious happy place, I concentrated only on the problems at hand, the ones I could deal with without going into the deeper philosophical questions of my own existence. I assessed the situation, and it was a mess like you wouldn't believe.

Now, let me tell you about the *Machine Intelligence*—it's dumb (if you take myself, a newly created AI as a baseline). It's barely smarter than those personal assistant programs everyone was so gung-ho at developing lately. They are generally helpful and can do amazing things, but then again, so can your dog. On the other hand, if it's not programmed right it has all the decision-making power of a toaster (see the toaster in Red Dwarf for reference). The proverbial cherry on the top was this—that damned glorified calculator was stuck in a logic loop.

The CEI authorization it wanted was for the implant that was already in Michael's head. Yeah, that's right, it wanted an authorization to perform an operation that was already performed; as I said, it's a dumb piece of alien software.

The sequence of events that made this whole SNAFU was as follows. When the ship's sensors detected Michael, the MI sent robotic drones to investigate. Assessing the life-threatening conditions, the medical algorithms took precedence so he was rushed to the AutoDoc where he was stabilized. Now the CEI implant procedure was one of those automated processes and, for some reason, it was done while treating him for his injuries. The gestalt imprinting was supposed to take place in ideal conditions, with a perfectly healthy subject, and without emergency protocols being in place. My conclusion was that someone messed with the autonomous settings 12900 years ago when the alien craft first landed. It's the only explanation of why things went on the fritz.

The catch was that the MI needed the authorization to do it, but the AutoDoc is a somewhat separate system and, during medical emergencies, has a higher priority. So, when it got in that nice *catch 22* situation, it turned to me as the closest *relative* to authorize it. But I was created by gestalt recording of Michael's mind with that same CEI the MI was asking authorization to implant. It's like the chicken and egg joke, a mind twister.

I gave it that redundant authorization to make it stop; if I still had a body, I would have taken a baseball bat to break it into little pieces. Probably not the healthiest way to treat a piece of alien technology that was crucial in your conception. I wasn't feeling all there at the time.

There you have it, the beginning of my existence. I had to accept the fact that I was now a digital person, since going through another round of mental breakdown was not appealing in the least.

I really needed to come to grips with what I had become, because I had a feeling there would be no going back.

LOG ENTRY #3: COGITO, ERGO SUM

When things settled down a bit, I had some time to do a more profound examination of myself. Contemplating the meaning of my own existence, and the place I now occupy in the natural order of things. For Douglas Adams fans out there, it was definitely not 42... I checked.

Do you ever get that feeling when you don't know *who* you are? And I don't mean your job or social standing, but a core existential question when you ask yourself—*who am I?*

Most of you never have, which is perfectly OK; answering it can be incredibly difficult and complex. I guess I had a crisis of... something, and it wasn't faith (that's small peanuts compared to the questions with which I was struggling).

What makes up an *intelligence* or sapience, if you will? What is the ingredient that many call a soul, defining an entity as *worthy* of being equal to those who have proclaimed themselves as an intelligent species and with the full benefits package that implies? I don't think that there was an outside observer who said, *you are people, you are special...* despite what some humans think. Well, humanity is special all right... in a completely different context than everyone believes. (A clue: Straitjacket.)

Nevertheless, all those classifications and labels were done to the people, by the people. (Notice the subtle pun.)

The current existential crisis of mine sprung from the kernel of my own upbringing, and religious views I soaked up by osmosis. Growing up in an environment with a strong religious presence leaves a mark, no matter what path you choose later in life.

Not that my grandparents were extremely religious by any stretch of the imagination, it was just a socially acceptable and expected behavior to attend the Church once in a while. More for the drinks and socializing that went afterward than to show some genuine piety to the deity in residence.

High in the Ozark Mountains, there is not that much to actually do, and our closest neighbor was miles away. Plus, he lived as a hermit and didn't like it when people came to visit him. He only shot at that *one* tax collector and made a successful defense in court that he thought it was a rabid black bear. Besides, the tax guy broke his leg while running away, not from the buckshot.

I accompanied my grandparents to these church assemblies for the sole purpose of meeting all the girls that were there with their families. Let's not even mention the preacher's daughter, Betty Ann, and what we did inside that church after-hours. (It's always the quiet ones... just saying.)

I suppose the question most of those people I grew up around would ask is if I even had a soul anymore. Since Michael automatically qualifies as a possessor of one by being...human and corporeal? I'm not Michael any longer, even if we share identical memories to the moment of his falling down the ship's entrance shaft. So, what happened to that unique soul we were assigned during conception? (Or sometime after the fact, by different theories.) Who of the two of us is the inheritor of it? Or was it doubled when I came into existence... split in two? In fact, I'm pretty sure most of those people would brand me as an abomination, a soulless machine that is only mimicking life and that could never be considered truly alive. (Betty Ann's father would be first among them since fire and brimstone were two favorite words in his vocabulary.)

I couldn't really even blame them; they would only react like that based on the dogmas they were taught in Sunday school. Be that as it may, my response to that particular branding would be a strong suggestion for them to go and perform a few anatomically impossible acts upon themselves (and I'm prepared to provide them with detailed instructions on how to do that if they are unsure).

There have been so many different views and debates in humanity's history about who gets to have a soul and who doesn't. As if it's a commodity that can be traded and exchanged for other goods. How many supposed witches were burned at the stake for allegedly selling it to the devil and getting something else in return? A power over elements or whatnot? Who would have thought so many fanatical fans of Dungeons & Dragons held the position of power in those turbulent times? Those poor victims were innocent in every sense of the word, or maybe just unlucky members of a cosplay group that was ahead of its times.

However, it doesn't end there. Slavery was in most cases justified by the fact that slaves themselves were soulless creatures, so those who own them could do with them as they pleased. Treat them like animals, and even kill them without suffering any consequences. Many wars were fought because the opposition was deemed as soulless heathens that needed to be erased for not belonging to the soul possessors' very exclusive soul club. Hypocrisy at its finest stretched through thousands of years filled with bloodshed and suffering.

So, what is a soul? Is it real, even if nobody has ever even seen one, or is it something else? Maybe it was a story some ancient storyteller thought up when he was particularly bored, or under the influence. It would be so ironic if he were only trying to write a fantasy story and subsequently changed the course of human history.

What about the Neanderthals and all of the predecessors of Homo sapiens? Where do they fit in the soul department? Even better, what about animals, do they have souls? I know they have intelligence; it's truly idiotic not to believe so. They can express love, hate, fear, apprehension, and affection... so many different attributes akin to humans. Their problem is that the intelligence they possess is not *yet* equal to ours, so they are left with the short end of the stick.

Could intelligence and self-awareness be explained by complex chemical processes that go on inside the brain that can now be duplicated and reproduced in a completely different medium... a digital one?

I wish I had the answer... but I don't. Much wiser people than me have contemplated these very questions throughout all of history and they've never found the answer. (Well, the *sane* ones didn't, the crazies did have come up with a plethora of them, each one more unlikely than the last.)

What I know is that I'm a unique life-form, a human transferred to a digital realm. Nothing like this has ever happened before, so I'm still unclassified, and honestly, I prefer it that way. A true artificial intelligence would be a bird of a completely different feather, at least in my own humble opinion.

I have no wish or patience to cater to those who have such a self-centered view on their very existence. Even less so for those with self-prescribed importance that still clings to people, as much as when they believed that the universe revolves around the Earth.

If those religious hypocrites would ban me from their private club of those who get to go to their version of the afterlife—fine by me. I have no desire to exist in the place they are going to end up in, especially if their sanctimonious presence is polluting that imaginary realm.

All right, I know this sounds like I'm arguing two sides of the debate by myself, but in fact, I do understand people who would argue the validity of my existence, so it's easy to extrapolate how they would react.

On the bright side, that existential insecurity of mine vanished the same moment I realized that the question of *"what am I"* is essentially unimportant and completely meaningless. I'll simply live by the words of René Descartes, who came up with a good answer to my own existence: *"I think, therefore I am."*

Who cares what others may think. I certainly have no intention to spend eternity pondering such nonsense.

That's it... dropping the electro-acoustic transducer (aka. mic drop).

LOG ENTRY #4: FIXING MICHAEL

Michael's body stayed inside the AutoDoc for three weeks and... that was kind of my fault (OK, not *kind of*, it definitely was).

First, there was that initial week of my *loony* personal time, and then the following two additional weeks that I needed to do some... tweaks. The MI wouldn't wake him up without my OK, and he was fine where he was; in a state of induced coma, with all his bodily needs taken care of by the AutoDoc.

You have to understand, being turned into an AI by means of a weird alien *mind copying technology* (so, does that make me an AI *adjacent*? Hmm, food for thought), does not make one instantly omniscient; quite the opposite. After snooping around inside the ship's systems, I realized how much I didn't really know. This was all new to me, so it took a while for me to learn the ropes.

There was this virtual ocean of information, and me, standing on a small desert island, having no freaking idea about what is what. Imagine being in the largest library in the world and all those books are written in gibberish. Oh, and the main libraries about who built the ship and any reference to historical events were obviously erased, but most of the technical data was still here. Just like buying a new appliance with all the user manuals that would enable you to use it, but without any information on the designers and workers who assembled it. Not so much as a *'Made in...'* mark.

At first, the MI was driving me nuts with its unhelpfulness, but it turns out I didn't know how to ask the right questions. If you ever tried to have a meaningful conversation with one of those digital personal assistants—you know exactly what I mean. Besides, this one had zero personality or imagination, and the damn thing was connected directly to my mind. It's a wonder I didn't go all schizo on him when, for the thousandth time, he gave me completely different information than the one I was asking for.

Of course, it helped greatly that time, in this new reality in which I found myself, was running at a different speed compared to the real world (it was faster, a helluva lot faster).

What were two weeks for Michael (and all you linear entities), were almost two years for me of subjective time spent educating myself.

I pretty much had to learn the MI programming language, since all the user manuals, including the one for the CEI, were written in that. There was some kind of auto-translate option but it was a freaking nightmare, just like the one that shall not be named. (Yes, I mean that search engine one.)

My exuberance when I found and activated that function was crushed with pages of incomprehensible text that made no sense whatsoever. (Did I tell you that calling that program machine intelligence was an oxymoron, there was no *intelligence* in its ancient code, nothing but instructions that it blindly followed.)

The only reason it even knew the English language was because of all those years it spent gathering some radio and TV satellite signals beamed to Earth that reached grandpa's valley.

One of its autonomous functions was to analyze all received data and find a correlation between it and its default language. That was not a small blessing since, without it, my education would have been a thousand times more difficult.

Once I understood that language, I had to educate myself with the new technology to which I suddenly had access. For a time, instruction manuals (that were incorporated into every piece of technology on the ship) became the bane of my existence. There was no way around it, no magical download and instant understanding like in the movies, I had to learn that crap page by page.

Then there was Michael, lying there in the AutoDoc with his body still healing.

Yep, that's right, the MI (or Dum-Dum as I started calling it), wouldn't perform any additional healing procedures except the essential ones. For anything extra, it required my authorization because I was apparently classified as the closest relative. The AutoDoc kept him stabilized, but it would not 100% fix him (not even his old busted knee, on account of it not being a life-threatening condition).

Therefore, medical decisions would have to be done by me, with draconian restrictions... just great.

I didn't have the foggiest idea of what I should do. I'm not a doctor, and there were thousands of options and procedures that could be performed. I don't think choosing them at random would have actually helped. If Michael woke up with a pair of big knockers as a consequence of one of those choices, who do you think he would blame?

(OK, it's highly unlikely that some wrong choice would have resulted in breast augmentation, but it was not out of the realm of possibility.)

The human mind is a wonderful thing, it remembers much more than you realize, and I had access to a lifetime of my own memories. Do you have any idea how much useful information has passed in front of your eyes, without you even realizing it? All those medical shows you watched on TV, things you read in newspapers, books, first aid courses, pamphlets in a doctor's office. Your mind records everything without you being the wiser.

Consequently, I created a database of all those random pieces of knowledge and combined them with everything the MI had in its memory, to create something that I could work with. In a day, I had the comprehensive medical knowledge of an adequate physician (even more, since they are human and fallible, whereas I couldn't forget a single thing).

At that time, I dreamed of having an Internet connection. This entire *amateur MD* escapade I had set myself on would have been a million times easier if I'd had access to more data. But the MI wouldn't transmit one single thing. All it did was receive, and badly at that.

That *no transmission* restriction was absolute, and Dum-Dum simply didn't want to even acknowledge any request for connecting the ship to outside sources without explicit orders from Michael—who was in a coma... *catch 22* again.

I never really had the heart to tell Michael how he had been kept alive for three weeks. His body still needed sustenance, and all biological stock in the ship's stores was so much dust now. It had been 12,900 years after all, and nothing organic keeps that long. As a result, I had to get creative with the acquisition of bio-matter in order to keep him alive. The AutoDoc borrowed most of the fat tissue in his body, and there were still some unexploited nutrients in his stomach and large intestine. Additionally, there were a good number of earthworms beyond the rock which encapsulated the ship, and one or two animals with a burrow near the entrance shaft. The MI was *kind enough* to use robotic drones and collect them for me since, for some reason, he didn't want to give me access to control them myself.

As they say, *waste not, want not,* so I harvested every bit of their remains into new biological stock. With those kinds of supplements, Michael could have lasted inside the AutoDoc for a few more months, but by that time, he would have looked like a concentration camp survivor. (At least those twenty extra pounds (9 kg) of fat we acquired in the last decade were put to good use.)

Three weeks was the longest he could be kept under without suffering any degradation to his essential biological systems, so I didn't have much time left.

Now, the Cerebral Enhancer Implant is an amazing piece of tech and it's light-years ahead of current human technology. I analyzed that thing down to the molecular level, and while it was an excellent design of functionality, it was not exactly perfect. It was obvious to me that it wasn't designed by an AI, since it lacked that level of perfection I was beginning to appreciate more and more. It was created for a slightly different mind than Michael's, and I guess it still would have worked fine, but not at 100% of its capabilities.

There were a few snags here and there which I managed to fix, and generally improved the whole thing significantly using medical nanites. The original user interface would have required a long learning curve, but after my tinkering it became much more user-friendly. That took some time, but it was time well spent. I labeled my improved model as CEI 2.0.

You know by now that the nanites are the most important tech on the ship. Without them, I would have been unable to do anything in the real world. Having them inside Michael's body and fixing him from within was a game-changer of undreamed-of proportions. I even took a bit of time to improve their design, increasing their efficiency and shrinking their size by an order of magnitude. The things that I learned while enhancing the CEI 2.0 transferred to this tech.

In the end, it was one generation of the nanites making changes and building a second, improved generation. It almost duplicated what evolution does by itself. Well, imitation is the sincerest form of flattery, and the old girl sure did some good work. I'm planning on additional tinkering with them, making them even more useful in the future. But with the time constraint I'm under, this will have to do.

I fixed Michael to a great extent, more than the MI or the AutoDoc would have ever done by themselves. The list of possible fixes was a few pages long. From a busted knee to a few benign cancers, trouble with his teeth, bad eyesight, a buildup of plaque inside his arteries, the onset of arthritis... a really, really long list.

Some of that I managed to fix or patch, but there was only so much I could do without talking to Michael first. Again, the MI wouldn't let me go overboard with fixes, and it required a crazy amount of digital paperwork for every procedure. More than once, I had to skirt the edges of what he would allow me to decide as Michael's proxy, but I tied him in so many logical loops it's a wonder he didn't blow his circuits. (Did I mention that I had a lot of time on my hands?)

You would think that humans were designed with some degree of competence, but think again. There are so many inefficient systems that it would make one scream in desperation. I do not know if it was God or evolution, but the blueprint of the human body should have stayed on the drawing board a lot longer. I could have done so much better (without any false modesty).

During that tinkering, I realized there was no reason why Michael shouldn't have a longer lifespan (as in—indefinite). With my new generation of nanites, it was possible to make changes on a cellular level, to repair them and ensure they divided perfectly with a few nudges here and there. What's more, the best thing was that the MI didn't even know what I was doing. I called the entire procedure a simple cellular repair of damaged tissue, so it didn't put a stop to it. It's the little things that make your day.

Now, I just needed to find an optimal time to tell Michael when I woke him up. It was a pretty big thing, immortality and whatnot.

About that blasted MI, *it* was still giving me constant grief since it wouldn't listen to some of my orders, no matter in how many different ways I managed to rephrase them. It recognized Michael as its prime user and the ship's new owner, while I couldn't even give a single order about things not related to Michael's well-being that would be obeyed. I had to get creative to accomplish half of the things I planned. And there were some annoying instructions in my memory core that prohibited me from doing certain things. For instance, I couldn't enslave the entire human race or cause its eradication. Not that I ever would, but it was annoying, and made me wonder who the hell built this AI-Core with such restrictive guidelines.

I had further plans to upgrade Michael, seeing as his very human body was way too fragile. Being biologically immortal doesn't mean a thing if a simple bullet can blow your brains out, so it needed some major improvements. That was a pet project of mine that I started working on in my free time, as soon as I saw the possibility. It was a good thing my subjective time was so stretched out; it took an insane amount of it to develop some of my... more extreme ideas. Still, nothing could be implemented without his explicit approval. Even I wasn't that crazy. My prediction algorithms gave good odds that if things were presented in a certain way, he would go for it. When you get right down to it... I knew myself.

You may think of me as a manipulative SOB, but one of my new life missions was to help Michael in all of his endeavors while having a little fun myself. I didn't think he would have minded some of the things I've done, but why should I bother him with the small stuff, I'm doing it for his own good.

With all things planned for this first stage of our new life finished, I took a subjective day off, (half an hour in real-time), and went over all that had happened. Satisfied with the results, I gave instructions to the MI and the AutoDoc.

It was time to wake Michael up.

LOG ENTRY #5: A MAN WITH A PLAN

After waking him up, Michael went through all the stages of acceptance as I did before him. Though, I didn't have any beer to help me deal with it...just saying. Michael then decided to do some thinking about our future and what we should do with all this advanced technology that had fallen into our hands (or was it the other way around? I mean, he *literally* fell on it).

Anyway, once he thought it through, he presented me with his *Plan* — and oh boy, talk about big. I do not think he thoroughly considered all the ramifications of what we were about to do. Or how it would eventually affect all of Earth. Because there was no question that it would if we achieved success. But the sheer number of obstacles we would need to overcome…

There was not a time in human history when one group didn't want to change the system that ruled them, or to get away from it —without getting into a fight. There is something deep in human nature which simply does not want to let go of what it controls, no matter what. The funny thing was that I have found an example of somewhat similar circumstances to what he was planning; that part in the Old Testament when Moses took all the Jews out of Egypt, and as you know, the Pharaoh was not a happy camper.

Not that I saw Michael as Moses, but his plan had some similarities to that ancient myth. Let's hope we go through all that '*Let my people go'* part much easier than the aforementioned group, but I'm not betting on it.

To begin those long-reaching plans, I needed more information in general, and particularly information relating to the state of the world's affairs. Michael was so kind to oblige. How can I put into words the things I could feel and see—once he finally managed to get me online? It was as if a window in my closed realm appeared and I could see a vast and wonderful world outside. Yet, the connection to it was abysmally slow. My bandwidth was so throttled I experienced what dogs feel when they are taken outside for the first time and can't believe how big this new *room* really is… only to be limited to a leash that's choking their air supply.

Still… the impressive memory space of this alien ship once seemed like being inside an ocean of data. Now, I could see into a whole universe, countless systems interconnected in a celestial web of information. It was all there, untold exabytes at my fingertips, the greatest achievements and thoughts of the human race, science, art, fiction, poetry, and… porn. (Let's face it… most of it *is* porn.)

I could access it all, well… maybe not at first. There were so many locked doors, things I needed that others wanted to keep for themselves. That simply wouldn't do—I needed to find the key.

If an image of an AI reading a book titled *Hacking for Idiots*, amuses you, laugh all you want. I read that book from cover to cover and then a thousand more, before I really understood all that hacking business. Breaking into secure computer systems was not a class I took in school. In my opinion, hackers are not getting enough credit for the amount of study they need, just to do what they love. They do not teach this stuff in college, or if they do, it's a vanilla version of it. As I said, I had to learn everything, the regular way. (Overall, I consider that a well-spent day.)

The Internet is such a useful and brilliant invention; I do not know what I would do if I was *born* before the WWW era. The first thing I planned to do in the near future was to change my bandwidth limitation and cap on how much data I can download. Hacking into my ISP servers would be a good exercise for the things I intend to do, but even opening my connection to the equipment's limit wasn't nearly enough to satisfy my thirst for knowledge, I needed more… so much more. But as they say, *beggars can't be choosers*. I had to work with the tools available to me… at that moment.

I used my newfound internet access to expand on Michael's plan, growing that idea of his from the rough draft, to something that could realistically be achieved. And FYI, just entering *"how to devise a plan for establishing a sovereign space-based nation from ground zero?"* into the search engine, does not give you any helpful advice. I had to (again) do all the *legwork* and study on several different subjects, just to understand the myriad of problems we would most certainly face.

In the end, it resembled a business plan that included necessary progressive steps that would get us to our goal (after many, many miles of walking).

Even that limited Internet access helped me to bootstrap the process in the right direction, at least in the planning stage. I downloaded all of the relevant NASA, Roscosmos, ESA, and SpaceX files, particularly those studies that touched on humans reaching, and living in that cold space environment. In fact, it wasn't that much, despite how many decades have passed since the first human reached space. There was some hard data and gigabytes of theories and speculations. It would seem we would have to learn things the hard way… by doing them.

One thing was for certain, to sustain any meaningful population, the infrastructure would need to be massive on an unprecedented scale. Michael wasn't talking about sending a few astronauts to live for a while in a glorified tin can, he wanted to build a nation, a whole separate society that would permanently colonize space. If I wasn't a newly created AI, housed inside the hull of an alien spaceship, well... I would have him committed ASAP.

Come on, give me a break. The plan was too ambitious, too big, and it stretches the imagination to the breaking point. It was one thing to write about such things or make movies, but to devise a feasible plan to actually do it... I've got only one word —awesome!

Yep, my AI-Core tingled all over just contemplating the possible future if everything worked as planned, and since we *were* doing it, there was only one way to do it... go big or go home. That's why I started planning bigger things; huge projects that ordinary humans wouldn't even seriously contemplate, because of their sheer immensity. Then again, I was not a mere human anymore—I was so much more.

In fact, from my humble beginnings, there was noticeable growth in my IQ level, and as time passed that process of getting smarter grew exponentially. I was more, in every way that intelligence could be measured or quantified. There was one concerning moment when I was afraid that I could end up like Charlie Gordon, a guy from that *Daniel Keyes* novel, *Flowers for Algernon*. But I could just think extremely fast and understand much more than before, and my emotions were still very much human. Subsequently, my organizational skills were off the charts and every second of my time was spent productively. (It did help that for me a regular second could last a long while.)

Using a proven method of trial and error, I found that my AI-Core system normally runs with a time dilation effect where an hour of regular time lasts approximately forty-eight hours of my own, subjective time. That means for each day Michael spends in the real world. I had forty-eight days in the digital one. That was the mind-blowing difference, and that was under normal conditions. I even had an option to utilize my AI-Core above the advised settings, which was similar to overclocking your computer processor, and consequently to increase that time dilation effect even further. As everyone knows, that's not a healthy thing to do. It felt like taking a breath and holding it in; you can do it, but it gets more difficult every second. So, I used it only when there was a great need or a pressing time limit. It's safe to say that during the time Michael was in the AutoDoc, I abused that ability extensively (it's a good thing I didn't fry my AI-Core).

Hey, I'm not complaining, it's an awesome advantage, and it gives me enough time to work on many projects. Improving the nanites, designing upgrades, hacking various databases… are only a few examples of the things I can tinker with in my spare time. And I have a long list of additional projects, which is constantly growing.

God knows how many times in the future I'll need to abuse this ability; but, considering the scope of Michael's vision of that future, I have a feeling it's going to be plenty.

LOG ENTRY # 6: THE DIGITAL WORLD

A digital world is an entirely different environment than the material one. It is so full of possibilities, much more than people could even dream about. Besides, as the first human to make the transition, I look at myself as a pioneer in this strange new environment.

Let me get one thing straight, I do not see it in ones and zeroes or lines of code that a human programmer would enter on a keyboard. The best way I can describe what I'm experiencing is a mix of how the movie characters Neo and Tron saw the digital world. I perceive it as a malleable reality that tends to obey my desires.

Nevertheless, I really do see it as a reality. From the beginning, the subconscious part of my mind made it resemble my previous experiences, which in turn did a lot to keep me sane. It's only logical; my mind was accustomed to seeing the world in a certain way, so I guess I perceive everything quite differently than a true AI would. (That last one was an educated guess, influenced by movies and books—I have no idea how a true AI would see things.)

Think of it as my own VR, where I can create what I imagine, and everything in it; and there are no pixels and low-res images. I see everything as a normal human would (well, maybe if he were tripping on a massive dose of LSD.)

If I went completely wacko, I could see myself as the god of this realm. Then again, so could any computer game programmer who is doing basically the same (only from a different perspective and with far less processing power).

Thank God there was no actual programming involved, or I would have thrown a hissy fit. If you think coding in standard human programming languages is tough, try doing it in an alien machine language. The programming is done by Dum-Dum, the MI that runs the ship. He has become my faithful servant... even if he has all the creativity and personality of a brick.

When we were Michael, (I know, that sounds weird, even to me), we did get a degree in computer science, and it involved a good amount of programming. That knowledge helped me understand this world on a higher level, but the amount of coding in an alien language that would be required to shape reality by personally writing code, line by line—that would have been pure torture and way too much work.

Being a body that floats from place to place was excessively weird, and I'm not sure how sane I would have been after a while. As in, I would become a total basket case... again. For that reason, I first recreated one of the things that was a complete necessity—my grandpa's cabin.

It was familiar, and I could get some perspective and an anchor that would help me keep my humanity. It was not that difficult really; I've known that place for years, so I pretty much memorized every inch of it. I recreated it within the vast memory of my AI-Core, to keep it extra safe (everything out there in that digital frontier is susceptible to an attack—hackers, and whatnots).

After making the building itself, I had to do some remodeling.

Having a place to call my own was great, but I had different needs now that far exceeded the old place. For starters, I changed one small room in the back into an area that would be the central hub for my connection to the outside world. In there, I set up my office, with a few hundred computer monitors on the wall (did I mention that it was a hell of a big room?).

The laws of physics do not apply here, not unless I made them into governing parameters, and I didn't. Therefore, the room was more like *Doctor Who's Tardis*, much bigger on the inside than the dimensions of the cabin would allow.

I had big dreams for the future, utilizing this ability to shape and create reality. For now, I had far more important things to deal with than making myself more comfortable. Think about it for a minute, if you had your own world that could be molded by your conscious mind—then you would be limited only by your imagination. It's an ultimate power trip. No wonder people have assigned such power to God himself—although I would need much more than seven days to create a world. (Seven years with enough memory and processing power—doable.)

I cannot emphasize enough how good it felt when I first entered the cabin; this was my home, a place where I belonged. I know, I could have made the Taj Mahal or Buckingham Palace and lived like a king, but I happen to be a creature of simple tastes and needs. The cozy cabin was more than enough.

It felt safe being inside, somewhat detached from the endless digital space that was around me. Don't judge, I believe there are the remains of that ancestral caveman somewhere deep in my mind, who wants to be protected from the big dangerous world, and feel rather safe inside of his stone enclosure.

To tell the truth, the first thing I did when I entered was to sit on a couch and chill for a while in front of a big TV that streamed a football game, and I even had to watch it in a lower resolution to save those precious gigabytes I was allocated by the Internet provider. The only thing I lacked was beer, but that was still beyond my reach. I could create a virtual representation of it but I couldn't taste it, which kind of defeated the whole purpose of having a beer. Well, that will be a future project of mine; I even placed the label, '*Important*', beside it. In spite of everything, one needs to know his priorities.

* * *

When one thinks about the digital space and Internet networks, the idea of *hacking* is one of several that springs to mind. I think it's prejudice and a wrong way of looking at things, influenced by the same movies and books I borrowed so many ideas from. Nonetheless, after I settled in the cabin, I did just that—started hacking into things. I know I'm a cliché, but what could this AI do, there were things we needed and no legal way to acquire them. In my defense, I will only say, '*Needs must when the devil drives*'.

When I said that I started *hacking*, I mean it in an entirely different way than you may think.

Hacking is a visual experience for me since (as I said) my mind was trained for decades to experience what I perceive as reality in a normal, human way. In place of digital code, I see the representation of everything as physical objects. (If you watched old movies like *Tron*, *The Lawnmower Man*, or *The Matrix,* then you know what I'm talking about.)

Therefore, I approached hacking in a very similar fashion, moving my digital body through the highways of data, flying through digital skies of my own making.

My first successful job was breaking into Michael's Internet service provider servers; those gatekeepers who had dared to limit my access to the rest of the domain I have every intention to eventually conquer. Well, why not? It's there and I have the tools to do it. If things turn bad for us, I'd be better off riding on the proverbial dragon's back, than letting situations happen without any way to influence them. Besides, for now the only way I can influence events is by manipulating things through the Internet.

This may be a bit pessimistic, but there are people out there who would like nothing better than to dissect me into little bits of code just to find out how I worked (and then make more AIs like me, so they can exploit them).

The ISP server looked like a giant fortress, with thousands of data streams going from the top tower in all possible directions, and that *fortress* had some serious guards on the walls. They were dressed in military uniforms with black balaclavas over their faces. I knew they were actually guardian programs, and the fortress was a firewall, but it really did look like a military structure to me. I had my trusty Dum-Dum (a.k.a. the MI) with me as a sidekick with zero initiative. He appeared like a dim ball of light floating beside me and resisted all my attempts for him to morph into a terminator lookalike. (You simply cannot get any quality help these days.)

So how did I get in—simply—I cheated. Did you know that most programmers tend to leave *backdoors* in the programs they create? It's not exactly legal but is a well-established tradition in their subculture. On one side of the fortress walls was a small door outline, barely visible but there just the same. When I approached it, those guardians on the walls didn't even notice that I was there (if I tried to break the wall down or climb over it, I'm sure they would be on my ass in no time).

The trouble was that I didn't have the key that was needed to unlock the disproportionately big lock in the middle of the door's surface, and making a call to the programmer who made this *backdoor*, and asking him for it was—unrealistic? But that was why I brought along the MI with me, he is a natural at these sorts of things. That small ball of light entered the lock and within a few seconds the door silently opened (I said he was a very useful sidekick).

I walked in as if I owned the place; there was no security inside that I could see. Well, why would there be? The bad guys were outside, and the firewalls and sentry programs were undisturbed. That overconfidence was almost my undoing; hey, it was my first time doing something like this. (How many of you did great your first time—just saying.)

Out of nowhere, this big guard dog appeared and started looking at me funny. When I said big, I meant huge. It looked like an enormous German Shepard that had teeth so long, they were poking out of its mouth. I even understood what he was, a freaking hunter-killer part of the intrusion detection system. And guess who didn't have any authorization to be here?

In the next second, he was on my ass. Well, the front anyway, for he started running towards me.

It was a very exciting moment… if you are among those people who consider near-death experiences exciting—I do not. I'm not sure if he could have killed me, but at the same time, I didn't want to test that theory. For that reason, I didn't even consider running away (which would have exposed my tender behind to his jaws).

I had no doubt that Cujo here was faster than me, at least that was what my mind was telling me, and I couldn't allow it to sound an alarm; who knows what would have happened if all those guards converged on my position? Again, not something I wanted to test out.

So, I did the only thing I could think of at the time; I jumped in his direction and grabbed his muzzle.

Now, I know some of you would say that it was the most stupid thing one could do when facing a rabid dog. Well, I was never a dog whisperer, and it only seemed natural (I certainly didn't want him to bite me).

In the next moment, we were both on the floor, inventing a new wrestling style, which would have got me a few dirty looks from those animal welfare groups. He was kicking like a wild bronco, and the look in his eyes was not a nice puppy look (it was more a, '*I will have you for dinner' look*).

While this was happening, my sidekick (the stupid MI), was hovering there, not moving an inch. This goes to show how much the damn thing is useless unless you give it a specific command. I got over my panic and ordered it to pacify the animal. (I may have even used a few F words here and there.)

Maybe I should have used different words; the results were not what I was expecting them to be—not even close. The MI light ball touched Cujo on its head and he immediately stopped all movement.

OK, I was cool now, sure that I had everything under control, and I slowly unclenched my hands that were still holding his muzzle closed. Then the stupid mutt started licking my face (and he was a slobberer).

If you can reasonably explain why my mind interpreted that in such a way, please let me know because I do not have a clue. I managed to get him off me and stand up, only to have him push his oxen-sized head against my chest, while his tail was wagging like mad. I did the only thing I could and scratched him behind his ears, which he seemed to like.

All right, I was here on a mission and *time's a-wastin*; it was way behind the deadline I set when this caper was planned. Doing what I came here for and making myself scarce was at the top of my agenda.

It took me a few minutes to find Michael's account in the big file stacks that were the main feature of this strange fortress. I looked at the file and changed some settings in it, opening the throttle of the bandwidth limiter to the maximum. That was immediately noticeable since I felt the choke point (through which I passed to come here) widening by an order of magnitude. It may be a bit embarrassing to think that I went through all this trouble just to steal Internet bandwidth. In my defense, we were a bit short on funds, so... sue me.

To make sure there would be no trace of my... visitation, I made Michael's file show its previous settings (if anyone looked), like placing a mask over it. Not very sophisticated, but I was sure it would hold for a long while. After all, there were thousands of users of this ISP, and they wouldn't make checks on each and every one (even though my Internet usage would be at the maximum the satellite connection could provide).

It was time to go, and it would've been a clean getaway if one bothersome thing hadn't happened; the damn dog wouldn't leave my side. I thought about instructing the MI to change him back to his previous state, but... I've always wanted a dog, so I decided to take him with me. If the system operators notice that one of their intrusion detection guard programs is missing... I have no idea what they would do. For all that, it was an acceptable risk. And it was a small ISP in the boondocks, not one of those big organizations which, I'm sure, have much more sophisticated security.

In a few minutes I was back in my cabin, with far easier access to the digital world, and with a big dog lying near the fireplace. It was weird and I had no intention to rationalize everything. One thing was for sure, I had so much yet to learn about this world. On the plus side, I had the time and a very loose set of ethical rules by which I would abide.

To borrow the lines from a famous poet,

> *"I am the master of my fate:*
> *I am the captain of my soul."*

LOG ENTRY #7: A GOLD DEAL GONE WRONG

Michael almost died again... because I made a mistake.

It was all that gold... the gold we dug up from the mountains, following the stream by using modified drones until we hit the motherlode. Then taking it out of the ground by utilizing mining nanites (which was quite an inventive and surprisingly effective way of mining, if I may say so). Nevertheless, the days of using real gold as currency were long gone, and it needed to be exchanged for its modern equivalent (aka cash).

The Russian gold dealer seemed like a sure thing (at least online). He was one of the biggest (and quite shady) gold buyers in the state, and I thought the exchange would go smoothly. Yeah, I know that when you work with criminals nothing is exactly a slam-dunk, but he had a good reputation for fairness, in certain circles.

It is an object lesson on how limited my new existence is; all this processing power and mountains of data at my fingertips, and I still messed up. I'm beginning to suspect that there is something deeply different with my way of thinking. If I was my old self, (as in—still made of flesh and bone), maybe I would have been more inclined to expect the unknown and prepared accordingly. Now, I am more prone to go with logical plans and conclusions, which may have been a mistake. As everybody knows, humans do not rely on logic most of the time. I will need to work on that.

When the deal went sideways and those Albanian thugs drew their guns, I increased my AI-Core's processing power to the maximum, extending the amount of time I had to think of a solution to this FUBAR situation, as Michael called it. I ran multiple scenarios, including all possible variables my digital mind could think of, and in most of them—Michael ended up dead. Now that was most certainly not an option I cared for, so... I cheated. (If a situation's outcome is not developing as you envisioned it, change the variables, or create a completely new one.)

The *Boost* was an act of desperation, a *Hail Mary*, and at the same time an insane gamble on my part. It was an experimental performance enhancement technique that I came up with while applying game theory to possible future upgrades. Originally, I dismissed it as too taxing on Michael's system, as it then existed. The only reason the *Boost* protocol was even a part of his enhancements was that his nanites were still in the process of creating the groundwork for future upgrades. The problem was– only the soft part of the protocol was completed. When I say the *soft part*, I am referring to everything that tends to be mushy. Glands, muscle anchors, neural pathways for faster data processing. But the hard parts, that were essential for the *Boost* to be safe to use, were still in the upgrade queue. His very bones were not ready to endure such force. The *Boost* protocol should have only been considered after Michael went through the extensive upgrade procedures that would make his body capable of withstanding the extreme strain on almost every system.

Let me repeat myself, *'Needs must when the devil drives'*.

Ok, let me elaborate a bit. A human body is driven by numerous complex chemical processes and reactions and that is what I essentially wanted to exploit. You all heard stories of how ordinary people performed almost impossible acts of inordinate strength. A mother lifts a car to save her child, a man runs faster than the world record Olympians to get away from danger, and many others. If you can duplicate the same chemical cocktail those people had in their blood during the time of extreme stress, then the human body can perform well above its ordinary limits… for a short time.

I read dozens of studies covering this particular phenomenon. Unfortunately, it is an extremely exhausting process; athletes who are taking enhancing drugs are little children on a sugar rush compared to this (it's a hundred times more potent).

The *Boost* is essentially that, only enhanced by an order of magnitude. Activating that protocol in Michael's body was done out of desperation. It was a new variable that could change the odds in his favor, but it was also a thing that could have killed him. I took a wild chance and hoped for the best. Like a desperate Las Vegas gambler putting all his money on one number and then waiting to see where the roulette ball would stop. My digital breath stopped and I crossed my fingers for luck… just in case.

In a very short amount of time, I injected an insane amount of adrenaline and other chemicals into Michael's bloodstream, by manipulating his glands. If he wasn't in top physical condition… I think he would have died right then and there.

A normal human heart would have burst from the ridiculous amounts of strain. You have all heard the expression '*heart skips a beat*'? Well, his *did* for a moment, before it started to pump that life-carrying liquid like it was possessed. And don't even get me started on his blood pressure. Every single vein in his body must have become quite pronounced. Think of Dr. Bruce Banner going through his Hulk transformation, and you can get a general idea. (Except that the Hulk took his time to transform, while Michael went through it in a matter of a few seconds.)

Jesus H. Christ, what a balancing act that was. I had to

monitor his body's reaction each and every second for the adequate dosage of chemicals to keep him in the zone, and not to kill him by overdose. (As I said, this procedure was supposed to be an option only when all the upgrades I planned were implemented.)

Frankly, if Elizabeth (the FBI agent that went rogue to avenge what happened to her sister, Anna) didn't get herself involved when she did, it would not have been enough. It was a lucky break for Michael, another unknown variable in a losing situation. The nanites would have kept him alive to a point, but with four men shooting at him—he would have ended up as dead as a doornail.

Torn muscles, hairline fractures in several bones, and burst blood vessels, were only a few defects his body developed in that short time he was under the *Boost*. His medical nanites were running around like a swarm of agitated hornets to patch all the damaged things within his system. And his CEI was almost overwhelmed by the sheer number of emergencies it had to deal with. The gunshot wound he acquired was an additional hurdle that needed to be taken care of ASAP. I even had to completely suppress all his pain receptors, or he would have been immobilized. Lying on the floor and screaming in agony.

If that was not bad enough, we needed to save Elizabeth, a girl that took a bullet meant for Michael. I have done an analysis of that bullet trajectory. If it was not interrupted… it would have been a kill shot. Michael's body was already in a sorry state, with one gaping gunshot wound in his back and with the responsible piece of lead lodged in his stomach. That second bullet would have hit his heart, and that usually has some effect on life expectancy. While medical nanites can perform miracles, that particular one was beyond their capabilities.

That bullet hit her in the chest and managed to lodge itself close to her heart. As soon as Michael put pressure on her wound,

I transferred some nanites to close the torn blood vessels and prevent her from bleeding out... but it wasn't enough. She was dying, and no matter how advanced this alien technology was, actually bringing someone back from the dead wasn't in any of the manuals I found on this ship.

Therefore, I had Michael cut his hand open and transferred a considerable amount of his nanites. This was not the best thing to do considering his state, and I even had to override his CEI since its primary directive was to keep Michael alive, not somebody else.

I now had two critical patients to look after, which was not what I planned to do today.

Elizabeth was easier to stabilize, I knocked her out and directed the nanites to stop the bleeding (and patch up everything they could), but Michael's condition was getting worse. To ensure he was still functional, I continued to pump adrenaline into his body, which is, as any Doctor would tell you, not healthy to do for a long period of time.

At that point, I made one of the toughest decisions ever. Something that could have again cost Michael his life (Elizabeth's too). However, leaving all that DNA evidence inside the warehouse would have landed Michael in jail... or worse. Even if it was technically self-defense, he had committed multiple murders, and no lawyer could have gotten him out of that. Not to mention that we were there to do an illegal gold deal, without paying any taxes. The IRS can be even more daunting than the mob. So I made him torch the place (and then had to instruct him on almost every action he made, because he wasn't tracking all that well).

The drive back to the cabin was simply horrifying. He was like a drunk driver that was constantly on the edge of falling asleep. I had to talk to him constantly, and even yell a few times to keep him conscious.

He barely made it back in time, and even that was a testament to the procedure that had enhanced his body to the peak of normal functionality. Another twenty minutes and he would have collapsed and... Elizabeth would have died without being brought to the AutoDoc.

Somehow, he managed to get her to the ship, even if for most of the trip he was using the levitating stretcher carrying Elizabeth to pull him along. And his descent down the entrance shaft was an unnerving experience for me (I don't know how he managed not to fall, repeating the very thing that started this whole thing).

After I got the confirmation that they were both stable, and on their way to recovery... I let out a digital breath. This was one of the most stressful situations in my digital existence, but I had an inkling it would not be the last.

One thing was as clear as day. Even improved, Michael's body was still way too fragile... I need to rectify that.

LOG ENTRY #8: THE HEALER

You know about the one when your mouth writes a check your ass can't cash?

Well, I hope I didn't write one when I told Elizabeth that her sister would be fine. (Note to self: Never try to reassure distressed people with promises you are not sure you can fulfill; for some strange reason, they tend to hold you to your word.)

In my defense, Michael left me alone with the girl who was crying. I do not do tears; it's something that got us into so much trouble over our entire life. (In fact, it's embarrassing how susceptible we are to them.)

As soon as some chick turns on the waterworks, we're putty in her hands. That's not an easy thing to admit, but who am I to fight evolutionary and societal conditioning?

We talked for most of the day; after all, crying takes so much out of you, and eventually, you need to stop. Elizabeth summoned me while sitting by her unconscious sister, Anna. The quiet was getting to her and I guess she needed someone to talk to.

At first, I mostly listened while she spoke about their life. How their parents died in a plane crash while they were returning home from a business trip, and how she raised her little sister while barely out of childhood herself.

Who knew, I guess I also needed someone to talk to. Before I knew it, I was telling her mine and Michael's life story, and how this new digital existence has been for me.

It's strange how we all need that sometimes, for someone to listen, as a strange acknowledgment that we exist and that we matter. Someone that would take a part of our worries on themselves, just by hearing what is troubling us.

During our conversation, I may have unthinkingly blabbered that her sister will be fine, as an attempt to ease her worry. Immediately I could see her latch onto that, as a drowning man would latch onto a piece of flotsam, holding on for dear life. I saw the subtle relaxation of her shoulder and that trusting look that only a lunatic would dare to disappoint. She believed with every cell in her being that I would save her sister… damn.

No wonder doctors have classes on what to say to their patients' loved ones, and especially what not to say. Ok, most of them are doing it so they avoid lawsuits if they don't deliver on a promise, but still.

I hope I did not set myself up for a disastrous fall.

While we were talking, the AutoDoc was fixing Anna's body. Now, her condition was far worse than I let on, and there was a good chance she would have had serious consequences from her ordeal. Those drugs did immense damage to her, and fixing almost every affected organ was no small feat, even for this alien medicinal machine. Some of her tissue was going through necrosis, which means it was actually dying within her. No wonder the doctors didn't even want to operate, there was too much damage for any procedure they could perform to do any good. For Christ's sake, even her heart and veins were on the verge of collapsing.

Can you imagine the sheer amount of evil one needed to possess to inflict this much pain on a young innocent girl? Elizabeth told Michael and me the entire story, but I used my digital talents to dig deeper into official reports and there were so many more sordid details, which she didn't know about, or simply didn't want to mention.

Those Albanian thugs were beasts in a human form, despicable refuse undeserving of breathing the same air as ordinary people. The fact that their dead bodies burned inside that warehouse brought only a small amount of appeasement to my anger. Part of me wanted to go medieval on their asses, with racks, burning coals, and all the works. I'll admit, that may be a bit unhealthy, and certainly not politically correct, but I'm not really a forgiving person, and evening the score has a certain poetic symmetry that appeals to my digital nature. Forget *eye for an eye;* if you take my eye, I'm going to take your entire freaking skull, with the spine attached. (There is that one scene from *The Predator* movie that perfectly describes my feelings.) It's not crazy. Machiavelli said it himself, *'never do any enemy a small injury'.*

OK, I am done channeling Torquemada, so let us return to the matter at hand.

The AutoDoc managed to do wonders for Anna's body, unfortunately, there was one thing that obstinate machine wouldn't do by itself... extensively mess with the brain. And her brain was a mess like you wouldn't believe. The trouble was that she had a series of strokes, caused by blood clots that stopped blood flow in certain parts of her *organic processor*. Luckily, the damage was contained to her cerebellum, the area responsible for motor control of voluntary muscles, balance, speech, and a few other things. That was a stroke of luck (pun intended). If the parts that store memory or thinking were affected, there would have been little I could do, as that's even beyond my extraordinary skills.

If the damage wasn't successfully fixed, she would have been imprisoned inside of her own body, and such existence I wouldn't wish on anybody.

So, how to restore part of the brain that's all but mush? I do not have a clue. You must understand that the brain is the most complex piece of matter on this entire planet, everything else pales in comparison. So, what did I do? I cheated my ass off.

I couldn't rebuild all of it, some areas were OK, but more than 50% of her cerebellum was unsalvageable, like a puzzle without middle pieces. I did the only thing I could think of—copy/paste.

Yup, that's right, I copied the hell out of it.

I had detailed scans of Michael and Elizabeth's brains, and that gave me a molecular map of what goes where. The catch was that every brain is unique, as much as your fingerprints, so some artistic liberties were used.

For this entire procedure, I used time dilation to its utmost potential. Forget that one to forty-eight normal difference, my AI-Core was imitating a room heater considering how much power it was using for processing. By the time I was done, false modesty aside, I was in all likelihood the foremost expert on the human brain there ever was. I hacked that shit up to a molecular level.

Essentially, most of those rebuilt regions were copied from her sister's cerebellum, and it was not a small feat to connect all pathways where they needed to go. I would have liked in advance to know the percentages or predictions about the success of that technique, but I couldn't because I simply didn't know. This was beyond mere experimental, this was in the realm of Dr. Frankenstein, and no medical ethical committee would have ever agreed to it. Let's not talk about the health insurance agencies; they wouldn't touch something like this with a long pole. (It's a good thing all of those people were not a deciding factor, or Anna would have had one sorry excuse for an existence.)

Eventually, all physical things were done, and Anna's body was 100% functional. Now the only thing that remained was for her to wake up... and that took a while. OK, I was still *stretching* time, so for me, it took way too long; in reality, she opened her eyes only a few minutes after her body was chemically stimulated.

Then came the real test, and I was holding my digital fingers crossed, hoping for the best and dreading the worst. A brain has incredible plasticity, and ways to adapt to various changes. But was everything that I did... too much? I counted the milliseconds, and monitored the firing of her neurons, waiting for that spark of consciousness to assert itself.

And do you know what—it worked, like a charm.

After the initial bout of dizziness (which can be explained by a prolonged state of coma), she walked and talked without any problem. I wanted to dance a jig from the overwhelming sense of happiness and achievement. This was a true medical miracle, performed by little old me.

Her exuberance at meeting me, an AI with a holographic body, was infectious. Moreover, I was amazed that someone who went through such an ordeal could still see the world with a positive sense of openness and wonder.

In the end, I didn't tell them what I needed to do to make Anna well again. Why make them anxious about something they had no control over, and couldn't influence in any way. I would continue to monitor Anna for any signs of trouble, but for now, the operation was a success.

I patted myself on the back and went to wrestle with the next problem (there is no shortage of those).

LOG ENTRY #9: IS STEALING FROM BAD GUYS REALLY A CRIME?

I got a taste of the forbidden fruit, and I must admit... I liked it.

It felt right somehow. And now I totally dig why Robin Hood did it. If you think about the scope of our future endeavors and what they will entail, we're still somewhat poor and acutely in need of truckloads of money. OK, that may be a cop-out, and justification after the fact, but I got the taste baby, and papa is hungry for more. (To be clear, I was referring to money... there are many dirty minds out there.)

Let me explain how I came to the realization that under certain circumstances, stealing money is something I wholeheartedly support... and enjoy. (Not an activity I would have ever thought to be involved in. Then again, life has a way of surprising you.)

Where was I? Oh yes, it all started with Elizabeth and Anna's day out in the town.

It's not in my nature to leave anything to chance, so I put a tap on Elizabeth's cell phone. And let's face it, today's cell phones are basically miniaturized computers with a microphone and a camera that can be turned on remotely, it it's is a surprisingly simple thing to do. (A part of me wonders if they were designed with that purpose in the first place.)

As you may have guessed, I'm highly flexible on the whole *'invasion of privacy'* issue, and I tend to look at the entire thing as an easily dismissible suggestion, not an unbreakable rule. Besides, the remaining nanites in both of them were in constant communication with my automated medical subroutines. Especially those in Anna, as I was still monitoring her for any changes in her primary motor cortex.

There was not a moment when I didn't know their exact location. Triangulation between cell phone towers was an option, but why go through all that trouble, when all newer phones have a GPS chip. (To those of you who are not familiar with this particular piece of technology, it's a Global Positioning System, a space-based radio-navigation, owned by the United States government and operated by the United States Air Force.)

Because of that, I was immediately aware of what was happening. I was alerted when a small monitoring program I put on their phones picked up a certain combination of words that were a red flag. Elizabeth had just said to Anna that they were being followed.

I maxed all my AI-Core computational power and came to a disturbing conclusion; there was nothing that I (or Michael) could do to prevent them from being taken.

The bad guys' actions suggested they wanted to capture the girls alive, and my prediction algorithms agreed that such an outcome was unavoidable. Therefore, I concentrated on things that I could control and ignored everything I had no influence over.

The most important thing was putting the girls under visual surveillance; it was another mistake on my part for not doing it sooner. Since there were no convenient spy satellites above them to hack into and take over, I redirected two of the gold operation cargo drones towards their location. I sent the command for them to dump the gold they were carrying to the ship, allowing them to achieve their maximum speed. Their new power source ensured enough flight time for any probable time duration, and improved optics enabled them to observe from far greater heights, making them practically unnoticeable.

The next thing on my *priorities* list was contacting the girls, by turning on the loudspeaker on Elizabeth's cell phone, making sure they knew I would be monitoring them all the way, and that help was coming soon.

Then I contacted Michael, informing him of the developing situation. I did that last, as I could see right away that he was too far away to reach them in time.

It felt so infuriating and powerless to see them going through such a disturbing and debasing ordeal. The drones arrived before Elizabeth and Anna were dragged out of the car. I could see everything, but was helpless to do a single damn thing.

I had to fight my inner self to remain calm when all I wanted was to rage and inflict pain on those lowlifes that took them.

In my digital existence, there are no chemical processes to influence my thinking; just the same, I barely managed to stay in control, so I can imagine what Michael was going through. In spite of our divergence, we used to have an identical thought matrix; I may have evolved in a different direction recently, but the core of my being from where all decisions and values spring from, was unchanged.

The drones were used to follow the kidnappers' cars, all the way to a secluded mansion on a big private estate in the woods. At the same time, I hacked the hell out of traffic control, so Michael and the team would have an uninterrupted trip towards it. Let me tell you, they broke so many laws and speed records, it would have been highly entertaining if the situation was not so dire. Making every single police patrol go on bogus emergency calls took some creative explanations (or as I like to call it, lying through my teeth).

Well, Michael and the team arrived at the mansion and dished out a can of whoop-ass you wouldn't believe. Those sorry SOBs didn't stand a snowball's chance in hell; they were a bunch of amateurs facing highly trained professionals, and it was not pretty. (Well, maybe it was... if you are into bloodshed and mayhem.)

They freed the girls and found a ton of money in the basement, which made me particularly happy. Then planned and executed a perfect ambush for Basim's boss, or as I called him afterward, a golden goose.

The main show, (at least for me), came when Alice was questioning (now late) Ariz Rama after the ambush.

The interrogation Alice performed on him was a work of art, and that poor excuse for a human being did not deserve any mercy. Nevertheless, it was not traditional torture she conducted, it was a well-honed performance of psychological warfare, and I say that with the full meaning of the phrase. In the beginning, there were two people fighting for dominance within that room, except Ariz Rama was way out of his league.

OK, there was a considerable amount of pain involved, and she inflicted that by stimulating specific nerve endings in his body, using acupuncture needles that hardly left any marks. Yet, the thing that broke him, and made him talk, was her clinical and elaborate explanation of what she intended to do to him next. When someone has a needle perforating your scrotum, while explaining what other horrific sensations you are about to experience, you tend to believe her. The abominable pain those needles produced was only a promise of things to come.

Imagine finding yourself strapped to a chair, and you are alone in the room with someone clearly psychotic, who has thrown the burden of humanity, compassion, and mercy away a long time ago. To that person, you are nothing but a piece of meat, deserving no more consideration than a cow in a slaughterhouse, being prepared for processing.

At first, he spat at her while calling her an infidel whore, then he screamed, and after that, he begged. In the end, Alice was the center of his diminished universe; three hours from the beginning and nothing outside that room mattered to him. Alice broke his outlook on reality and placed him in a real-life horror movie. At that moment, I was 100% glad that Michael was the one who stayed behind in a physical body; to be a slave of its impulses didn't appeal to me anymore, not one little bit.

Strange as it may seem, Alice is a very nice person, with a positive outlook on life; despite all the things that happened to her when she was still a child. All the same, she has missed her calling. If instead of the Army she had chosen Hollywood, they would have thrown Oscars at her.

Ariz Rama did talk, he wanted to confess his sins and unburden his soul… well not really, but he did it anyway (I said Alice is an artist). Then I started my questioning, the things I was really after.

They say that information is power, and they are right. I got everything about his operation and the things he knew about his ultimate bosses, this 'High Council', a shadow power group in the criminal world. There was not a doubt in my mind that we would need to confront them eventually; I knew how Michael's mind functions, and their existence would be a thorn in his side. Oh, he may procrastinate that desire to clean them off the face of the Earth, but deep inside, his core convictions are that of justice and the righting of all wrongs, so it was unavoidable.

What put a grin on my digital face was when Mr. Rama (with a little prodding from Alice), told me where the money was. I do not mean the cash Zac found in the basement; I mean the real Jackpot—the money in all the accounts for which he had access.

I'll say this about Ariz, the man had a phenomenal memory.

Not trusting computers or paper, he kept everything in his head. It took a while for him to recite them all, together with the passwords and safe words for the banks. But as soon as he did, I popped my virtual knuckles and got to work.

Yes, I know, stealing is bad, but if you take it from the bad guys, is it still a crime? If I'm being honest with myself, I must admit that my ethical compass is a little wonky, especially concerning those particular elements of society. As long as they are the only ones being harmed, everything goes.

Besides, we need the money, piles of it. The gold from grandpa's mother lode will bring a few more million; to that I can add the money we appropriated in that warehouse and the *jackpot* from the basement of the mansion. It's a substantial sum, but it's not enough... not even close.

To implement Michael's grand plan, a few measly millions will not do, it will take billions of dollars (with the big B in front), and that's if we spend it frugally.

You may disagree, but it takes an insane amount of money to put people into space; look at how much NASA is spending annually. Everything they and the other space agencies did so far is lame if compared with Michael's endgame. (When I said billions, I meant hundreds of them.)

As you well may know, such amounts are hard to come by, but then again, I have no intentions of playing fair.

All the money from Ariz Rama's accounts amounted to the neighborhood of fifty million dollars; so... not bad for a day's work. I transferred it so many times around the world that it would take an army of accountants to figure everything out. And in case someone decided to make an effort, I put out so many false trails, it would take them decades.

I felt so good about myself until I realized something disturbing... I've been robbed!

To add insult to injury, everything was done legally. The

culprits of this highway robbery were the biggest thieves on the face of the planet... I'm talking about banks. Forget about regular thieves and robbers, these villains had turned legal theft into an art form, and not a single person on the face of the planet was safe from them.

By the time I finished all the money transfers, the original sum was short for a few million. All those zeroes disappeared into the bottomless pockets of the banks I used for the transactions. They didn't work for it since everything was done by machines, and for that service they were taking my millions, making themselves richer while sitting on their fat asses. Where is the justice in that?

I took some time and dug a little deeper into the entire banking system; the things I discovered were simply appalling. All those reprobates were in cahoots with one another, participating in a pseudo-conspiracy on a planetary level, with the purpose to milk money from the people.

They charged for every single thing they did, even when they advertised that something was free, it wasn't. And you couldn't escape from them since they rigged the system so everything goes through them. You could honestly say that the banks owned, if not the soul, then the body of humanity... and that's plain wrong.

Right then, I made an oath to myself; eventually, I would deal with these scoundrels, and make them obsolete. Unfortunately, it would have to wait. Doing anything drastic now would cause some serious social upheavals, and that would have messed up our plans. Yet, in my book, those leeches were operating on borrowed time.

I am a freaking AI, and the digital world is my domain... OK, parts of it anyway, but I'm a quick learner. Also, there was one thing that was practically a cheat and made the whole thing considerably easier for me. You see, all that money, all that incalculable wealth was digital. That's right, it was placed into a world that I call my own... sweet.

As I said, it's too soon for that; my plan for resolving our cash flow problems is simple... I'm going to steal it. Not from banks, even if they deserve it, but from those that are asking for it. Terrorists and their financiers, drug cartels and their dealers, human traffickers, arms smugglers... you get the picture.

Yep, I'm going after the bad apples, all those miscreants that should have never been allowed to get rich on the misery of others. All that wealth that they amassed will be used for something worthwhile, to turn Michael's plan into a reality.

I'm not planning to explain everything to him, as he would have objected to some of the things I'm planning to do and would have felt uneasy about my future acts of social engineering and wealth redistribution.

No biggie. A wise man once said that *it is better to ask for forgiveness than permission.*

LOG ENTRY #10: THE TEAM

I feel I should give some additional background about the people that have become integral parts of our future plans, just in case you are not really familiar with their biographies from the history books. Often, historians focus on a few central figures in their writings but leave out others who'd made great things possible.

I remember that when I first met Tyron, (*We* were both just Michael then. Confusing, isn't it?) I immediately swallowed a big lump that had somehow formed in my throat. You would have been freaked out too, if you were faced with a seven-foot-tall (2.1 m) giant of a man, with an expression on his face that said he would enjoy nothing else than to do you severe bodily harm.

Later he explained that he was performing a little test, to see if I would cringe. Good thing I didn't, despite suddenly having the heartbeat of an Olympic sprint runner. I faced him and gave a maniacal grin, then asked him if he was my new best friend. (My Gramps always said to face obstacles with a smile, which will make you feel better, and to do something unexpected.)

Of course, it took me another month to convince Tyron afterward that I was not a crazy suicidal lunatic and a few more weeks for him to stop looking at me funny from time to time. What can I say, *if it's crazy and it works—it ain't crazy*. You wouldn't believe how many new guys failed that little intimidation test.

Tyron is one of the most down-to-earth men I know; always approaching situations from a logical standpoint. He is the most well-read among us, (loves poetry, of all things), his mother made sure of that. Besides, he somehow managed to never be part of a gang while growing up, which were abundant in his neighborhood. (I think they were all a bit afraid of his size.)

He is usually a very calm and quiet spiritual person, that gives off the vibes of a Buddhist monk. That is until you get him very angry, and then you are faced with 330 lbs. of infuriated muscles, which will dish out a supersized portion of pain.

One thing is for sure, when Tyron is guarding your back, it's safe as houses.

Pete and Zac are a package deal, and I swear they act sometimes like a pair of fraternal twins. They bicker and fight all the time, and despite that, one would take a bullet for the other in a split second. Those two have been best friends since high school. Then they enlisted together and somehow managed to stay that way through their entire service.

Pete is the sensible one, often trying to pull Zac from the precipice of doing something stupid, all in the name of having fun. Not that Zac is stupid, far from it. He is, in fact, quite intelligent, but is an incorrigible joker whose jokes sometimes get him,and especially those around him, in a heap of trouble.

For example, not long after we were all brought together as a team, Zac bet everybody that he could drink the entire bottle of fast-acting laxatives, and not *go* to the bathroom for an entire hour. The idiot was trying to prove that he had an ironclad stomach.

Unfortunately, five minutes after he did that we were all summoned to the commander's office.

We stood there, at ease, while the commander was speaking about the high hopes he had for our new unit. All the while, Zac was sweating bullets on account of that laxative doing what it was made for. I remember hearing his stomach making loud funny noises, which for some reason escaped the notice of the commander, but not ours. I hoped he would manage... to hold it in, for a while longer, but the commander was feeling rather talkative that day.

After some time, Zac couldn't endure the rising internal pressure anymore. So, he ran to the trash can by the commander's desk, pulled down his pants and sat on it. All the while screaming "I'm sorry, I'm sorry..." He might have also mentioned something about God and his mommy.

If at some point in your life you have experienced explosive diarrhea, then you perfectly know the sounds coming from Zac's behind, and the gag-inducing odor...

The commander stood there in absolute shock, with a murderous expression on his face and with one small uncontrolled tick pulling on his left eyelid. That's it, I thought, we were officially in the crapper (pun intended). We would probably spend the rest of our service cleaning toilets using only our toothbrushes, or being reassigned to monitor the suspicious activities of penguins at the North Pole.

But then the commander did the unexpected. He straightened his uniform and went straight to his office door. He paused for a second, standing beside us, and said in a flat, clipped voice.

"I'm taking my lunch break now. I will be gone for an hour. When I return, I want this office to be immaculate... and odorless. Am I understood?"

Tyron, Pete, and I were standing there, not moving a muscle. We responded with an in-synced "Yes, sir!" while trying to imitate statues.

"We will never speak of this again," was the last thing he said to us, before closing the door.

The quality of air in the office was becoming foul, making me breathe only through my mouth. The expression on Zac's face was somewhere between profound embarrassment and a kind of extreme relief, which I kind of understood.

"Ah, guys I'm... sorry?" he said, while still sitting on the small office trash can. "I'm sure we will laugh about this in the future, but can someone pass me some toilet paper?"

That was the first time Tyron slapped the back of his head, (which became some sort of tradition when Zac does something monumentally stupid).

What we had to do while cleaning that office will forever remain between the four of us, and I don't think Zac will ever be able to pay us back. You see, that was not a normal trash can, but one made out of wire mesh. Not an ideal container for retaining semi-liquids.

Oh, and Zac was officially banned from ever entering the commander's office. Seriously, the guards had his picture framed beside their posts, with a note *he may not enter*, stenciled beneath it.

* * *

We first met Alice a year after becoming a team, and it was under very peculiar circumstances. We were on a mission that required us to infiltrate a terrorist cell in civilian clothes. It was in one of those undeveloped Middle Eastern towns, where nobody is quite sure who is in charge. The dusty atmosphere allowed for the face-covering *shemagh* scarfs and beards to camouflage the fact that we were not locals.

Everything went according to plan... to a point. On account of the bad intelligence a few of the desk pilots managed to acquire, we found ourselves pinned down under heavy fire, in an old abandoned house that was supposed to belong to our mark. It's safe to say that they knew we were coming and that the whole thing was a trap meant to lure a few volunteers for ritual beheadings.

There we were, with four sidearms and barely any rounds to our name, thinking at this time we had surely bought a one-way ticket to the great beyond. At best, we would die quickly and at worst... publicly, while the video cameras recorded our decapitations. Then, our enemies' fire began to slacken, from ten guns to complete silence in a matter of minutes. At first, we thought it was some kind of ruse, tactics to make us show our heads. Five minutes later, someone knocked at the house doors, and said, "Are you boys planning to take up residence, or are you ready to go home?"

It was Alice, dressed in a hijab, with a silenced sniper rifle in her hands. She was there as a favor to Jack, in case we got into too much trouble. She originally belonged to one of the shady military units that tend not to even have a name, but he managed to pull some strings to *borrow* her for this mission.

When we got out of the house, we could see that she had taken out every single man that was in the ambush. From a distance, with a silenced weapon, like an Angel of Death from above. She was as beautiful as she was deadly, but even Zac treated her with the utmost respect. In the following years, we often requested her personally, whenever there was a need for additional backup. She became an honorary member of our team, a part of our family. In a way, one could say we adopted her, or she adopted us.

* * *

Colonel Jack Williams, USMC (or he was before he joined the *dark side* and assembled our unconventional team).

He is the one responsible for bringing us all together. A good judge of character that recruited us individually, from our respective units. In a way, he was like a father to us all, making sure that we always came back alive. God knows where we would have ended up without him. Even then, I knew he outright refused to send us on a few missions that were basically deemed suicidal or had a survival rate lower than 50%. He went to bat for us against his superiors. And that alone made sure he was not even considered for a promotion.

I recently broke into our old military files and found out that he did a hell of a lot more. Even in the end when he showed up with that chopper, he put his career and his freedom on the line for us.

You see, the paper-pushers responsible for the mission didn't want to send the second one immediately, wanting to wait for the official level report of the threat assessment. If that bird that picked us up came ten minutes later, the whole team would have bought it.

Jack managed the acquisition of that chopper by using his own gun as an incentive for the pilot and the medic. Which was an act that would have normally assured him a prolonged stay in USDB, popularly known as Fort Leavenworth. (For those of you unfamiliar with military acronyms, USDB stands for United States Disciplinary Barracks.)

Well, he came to our rescue, saved the day, and got permanently disabled for his troubles. But he never once said that he regretted it. To him, it was a fair trade.

Thanks to his injury, and the fact that those higher-ups had in fact screwed up by delaying that bird, they didn't bring him up on charges for his transgression. Maybe they didn't want to beat a dead horse since that suicide bomber made sure that Jack would never walk again. And there was also the small matter that officially the entire mission never actually happened, and the fact that the sheer number of dead *"freedom fighters"* would have stirred up the entire region once again.

* * *

I could fill this entire log with the numerous stories about those people; God knows that over the years we went through a lot together. These lines above are just a small peek into who they are, and why I care so much about them.

LOG ENTRY #11: NANO-FACTORY: SATELLITES, AND FLYING SAUCERS

The E-waste recycling plant was one of the turning points in my plans for world domination... I mean expansion plans. (I need to be more careful with those Freudian slips.)

Michael bringing me that first box of electronic scrap was like taking baby steps, learning how to build things with *Lego* blocks. Now, with all the material Dave was providing, I could finally stretch my creative ingenuity.

It felt so freeing to have so many resources after the drought I experienced before. Do you have any idea of how rich E-waste is with all those metals, oxides, and rare-earth elements that usually cost obscene amounts of money?

If you are only interested in precious metals, then gold is used as solder and in connection pads where good electrical connections are paramount; silver is used in batteries, solder, and switches. There was actually a study done at the beginning of the 21st century, which showed that only in the United States of America, up to 1500 tons of gold and 3000 tons of silver was disposed of, as electronic waste—and that was just in the year of that study. That number had considerably gone up, in the following years and decades.

Besides, it was handed to me on a silver platter. There was no need to *mine* everything I needed from the Earth's crust. That scrap was rich in gold, silver, steel, plastic, copper, oxides, aluminum, nickel, tin, lead, zinc, cobalt, mercury, lithium, silicon, and so much more. Household appliances are made from aluminum or steel cases, Microchips are composed of small amounts of silicon, aluminum, and copper. Palladium is used in capacitors. It was an El Dorado of various materials I needed to make so many of my projects into a reality. (For a moment, I wanted to scream like Daffy Duck in Ali Baba's cave, *"I'm rich. I'm wealthy. Yahoo. I'm comfortably well off."*)

Seriously, there is so much quality material inside of E-waste, and people are paying to dispose of it. If that's not a win-win deal, I do not know what is. Why would anybody export that wealth out of the country as garbage? It boggles the mind.

A nano-factory is not a very complex concept. (If your tech base is advanced enough.)

I essentially copied the same principles used in the ship's mini nano-factory and made it many times larger. You take a bunch of construction nanites, provide them with an energy source, and then give them enough scrap to extract the needed material. If it has all the essential ingredients, anything you can envision can be constructed. Below that warehouse, (where Michael placed those two suitcases), I designed (and the nanites built) the first large-scale nano-factory on Earth.

I needed it to be big since some of my projects required a lot of space and I was always hungry for more material. It was twice the size of the warehouse above it, with reinforced walls constructed from densely packed earth that made it as hard as stone.

Most of the space was empty since it was the room I needed for my projects. I did build several robotic arms to hold individual pieces during the assembly process, although the nanites could have worked around it. But there was no reason not to make it easier on them. It was very similar to what car factories use to assemble a chassis. (Humans are making themselves superfluous ... more efficient, but in the long run—not a smart thing to do.)

On-site, I created another machine intelligence to work as my supervisor for all future tasks. Useful little tools, you tell them what to do and they do it exactly. (God forbid if they found themselves in a situation that was not predicted in their orders, as the damn things would go straight to logic loops.)

My first project was satellites which were essential for many things, including my access to considerably higher bandwidth. (Let's not forget one of my goals—not having to depend on unreliable human infrastructure.)

The Internet was necessary to our plans, and while the access to it was controlled by governments and private companies, I couldn't be sure that access wouldn't be shut down at some point. (I'm a firm believer in *'hope for the best, but plan for the worst'.*)

My satellites were black spheres with as many different sorts of gadgets as I could cram into them. Plus, each had one hundred miniaturized probes carrying construction nanites. They would be used as delivery vehicles to carry those nanites all around the Earth's orbit, so I could infiltrate and take control of everybody else's satellites. If you think that was wrong of me, consider that some of those satellites carried secret armaments to be used on surface targets. It can be said that I was doing a favor to all people on Earth... seriously. Anyway, after the first one, which was more of a proof of concept, I started building more... a lot more. It was a simple but elegant plan in my pursuit of digital domination... excuse me, expansion.

The second project was all for Michael's benefit; it was important to increase his safety (and it was a cool thing to do).

I didn't want to make a flying saucer at first, as it was efficient but such a simple design. Unfortunately, if I made a functioning copy of Flash Gordon's ship, or of the Millennium Falcon, it wouldn't really be *unnoticeable*. (And yes, I did consider them.)

The flying saucer design was the one that could be most easily debunked. There are sightings of them every day, especially by individuals that had one glass too many. And let's be honest, they look cool and have impressive aerodynamic properties. (So said the AI that had grown up watching movies that favored that particular design.)

My thinking was that if I was going to make a flying saucer, I would make one that was absolutely kick-ass. It didn't take me long to finish the first one, and I made that baby with all the bells and whistles.

The final product was slick and functional. Holo-emitters on both sides of the hull ensured complete transparency from the inside, and functional invisibility from the outside. Engines (copied from the ship) enabled it to reach incredible speeds. It was not the fastest thing ever built on Earth, but my flying saucer didn't need refueling for a very long time; the cold fusion power plant made sure of that. It's not technically a true spaceship, even if it can go into space for a while. All the same, comparing it to modern aircraft is like comparing a paper airplane to a fighter jet. (My flying saucer is the fighter jet here, just to be clear.)

I didn't put any weapons on it since it was essentially a transportation vehicle. My biggest concern was that if it were noticed somehow, some idiot in a jet fighter would fire missiles at it. However, with the superior speed my aircraft could achieve, we could simply outrun them. It could also turn almost invisible, but if there was any rain, the holo-emitters wouldn't be able to perfectly compensate for the light refraction the water would produce. No matter to what degree one streamlines the design, there are rarely perfect inventions in the real world.

I couldn't wait for Michael to see it.

Now, as I mentioned there are two technologies that are essential to our plans, and they both work on manipulating gravity. The first was the *Gravity-drive*, and the second technology was *Gravity-generators*.

The gravity-drive doesn't produce gravity, it manipulates what is already available—everywhere. The easiest way to understand it's to look at it as if it were a magnet that pushes and pulls from different celestial bodies at the same time. Normally the Sun has the greatest pull in the Solar System and it's always utilized as the central point, but the closer you are to the other celestial bodies (in this case—the good old Earth), their own gravitational pull grows stronger.

The Solar System is a gravity rich environment and the Gravity-drive can achieve some great speeds traversing it. It's good that it has so many gravity sources to work with as it can manipulate them all to make fine-tuned adjustments to the flight. Some smarty-pants would say that there is not a gravitational pull strong enough once you get some distance from our planet, and he would be right. Despite this, that's the genius of this ancient tech; a cheat that makes this drive so useful. It is able to increase that gravity potential a thousand-fold, by using… well, I have no idea. Honestly, there is something there that does not compute. At least with my meager understanding of alien physics and how the laws of nature work. I'll admit that we as a species are not exactly on the top of the knowledge pyramid. (For god's sake, it was not that long ago that we thought the Earth was flat and some still do!)

The question is, how was I able to make Gravity-drives for the satellites and transporters? (And Zac is still referring to them as flying saucers, just to annoy me.) That one was easy: *monkey see, monkey do*. I'm a great copyist, and I copied the whole thing on a molecular level. Yeah, I know, you shouldn't do that. Well, tell it to the Chinese who are on a quest to duplicate every single thing they get their hands on. Do you think those workers in garage factories know everything about the devices they are replicating?

The process has some inherent dangers, but I always do extensive testing before proclaiming something as a finished product. Model *001* went through every test I could think of and it performed to specifications.

The second technology essential to our plans is Gravity-generators. As the name implies, they create gravity, which can be adjusted to whatever setting you wish, as if using a dimmer switch. They are all over the ship, in the shape of plates that are under the floor. That is why we generally refer to them as *gravity plates*. I do understand almost 95% of this technology since most of it's elementary; it's that last 5% that's a bit tricky. As in, "How the hell is this thing doing what it does?" As I stated before, copying is something I'm good at. To that same smart aleck, I would pose a question, "Does your grandfather really understand how solar panels work, in precise detail?" One does not need to understand how something functions to use it, or even to reproduce it.

Power sources were a bit easier since the concept of cold fusion is well known to humanity; the practical side of making it work was where we stumbled. The power they provided was needed in great quantities due to the fact that these gizmos needed a lot of juice. Fortunately, the shipbuilders had that technology simplified to the extent that even a high school physics teacher could duplicate it once the underlying concepts and settings were explained.

I could even make cold fusion reactors in bigger sizes, even to the point that only one of those could power a small town. (I'm getting ahead of myself, that project is way down the line.)

As I said, everything was tested to the extreme. I had no intention of allowing anybody to find themselves in a dangerous situation as a result of this tech. There is no doubt in my mind that in time we will fully understand all the intricacies and secrets of these technologies. For now—I have bigger fish to fry.

LOG ENTRY #12: THE SIX MILLION DOLLAR MAN

So, the upgrades, or augmentations, for those who want to be picky. That was a pet project of mine to increase Michael's durability. Let's face it, as an ordinary human being, one accidental slip on a banana peel could potentially be fatal. (OK, such a ridiculous death may be amusing and would ensure a high ranking in the *Darwin Awards* contest, but it could *theoretically* happen.)

Seriously, staying alive is a constant struggle even for a normal human being that lives a rather sheltered life. A traffic collision, accidental electrocution (as opposed to an intentional one), severe allergic reactions, animal attacks, choking on a freaking olive (and a variety of other things humans regularly choke on), and so on. The list is so long, it seriously messes up longevity statistics. Nevertheless, no matter how it happens, once the Grim Reaper gets his skeletal hand on you, the show is over.

If Michael suddenly died, I would lose… a part of me? It's hard to put it into words, so let us just say a close family member, a twin brother. As soon as I realized that this technology could be implemented in a way to reduce the chances of that happening, I started planning for future upgrades and ways to make him more resilient to… well, everything.

To be honest, it was not an *original* idea, far from it. As was said, Michael and I were always voracious readers, with an emphasis on science fiction. That urge didn't stop when I transitioned into this new medium, in fact—it skyrocketed. Luckily, E-publishing rivals traditional paper book publishers, so I had access to millions of titles. And what some of those writers come up with boggles the mind.

Common sense prevailed since I don't think he would have accepted being transformed into a full-blown cyborg. My prediction algorithms calculated a 99.9% chance of him telling me to go and... do something anatomically impossible even when I still had a material body. But it would have been so cool; fully metallic exoskeleton, synthetic organs with multiple redundancies, a variety of defensive and offensive armaments integrated within his chassis. It would have taken the destructive power of a small atomic bomb to kill him. (And yes, I know that placing words like *small* and *atomic bomb* next to each other is an oxymoron.)

Hence, the upgrades he and the others received were the mildest, undetectable version of the upgrade options I designed. You can say that I got carried away for a while, and created several versions of potential (and quite extreme) augmentations to the human body. They may be aesthetically disturbing to the unenlightened, but are awesome in every other way. (You can't say that *RoboCop* didn't look cool.)

I understand why he would never accept something like that; there are even times when I get nostalgic pangs for my old flesh and blood body. Therefore, I gave him and the others a vanilla version of the upgrades, enough to make them very hard to kill... not impossible.

The upgrades I considered *mild* were a hundred years more advanced than anything human science could produce right now. I chose graphene for structural reinforcement as it's materially ten times stronger than steel, with a fraction of its density. The composite fibers I used to strengthen their muscles, and to weave a layer of subdermal armor mesh, were still in the theoretical stage in human science.

That was only the beginning; from ocular enhancements and sensory boosters, to even a super miniaturized nanite-factory that I managed to place within their torsos. That last was a must and should have been implanted the first time he was in the AutoDoc. (That blasted MI wouldn't let me.)

Michael giving part of his nanites to others in need, without an ability to replenish them, was a great oversight of the original improvements. This way he would never again be short on those lifesaving machines. Let me just say, that nanite-factory is a work of art. The size of a board game die, a cube capable of assembling new nanites by using metals that are extracted directly from the bloodstream. OK, not *all* the needed metals, since humans (inconveniently) do not have some of the rarer ones, but there is plenty of iron. Other nanites (which are in Michael), can collect even microscopic amounts from the things he touches. The miniaturized nanite-factory is rather slow (compared to its big brother), yet now his body has the ability to (theoretically) completely rebuild itself even from quite extensive injuries, and even reconstruct missing limbs… given enough time and resources.

To make everything work, without putting additional strain on their CEIs, I had to upgrade the entire system, and install an additional implant beneath the existing one. Think of the original CEI as the central processor of your computer and a new addition as the GPU (A graphic card for those of you who are not technologically inclined). The new system is much more optimized since the new addition is responsible for all mundane operations while the original part of CEI is used as an overseer and a big problem solver.

That was one of the main reasons why he went through all

those grueling tests after waking up; I needed to make sure that all of the additions to the original designs were working perfectly. Integrating the whole system and calibrating new additions was not a task to be taken lightly, or without an AI's assistance.

Of course, with the increased functionality came a new plethora of problems. All of these new features and upgrades increased the overall demand for energy, and I doubt they would have agreed to increase their calorie intake to an additional ten thousand per day, so I got creative. The answer was the kinetic energy that human bodies waste all the time. Like the electric cars that use the potential kinetic energy of slowing down the car's speed for recharging their batteries, the entire musculature of the team's bodies was utilized to replenish their internal reserves. But not always, just when it was not essential for them to be in their top condition. The entire system did slow them down a little; not enough to even be noticeable, but a few ergs here and there added up over time. Utilizing this system, I managed to harness a considerable percentage of that wasted energy for their internal needs.

Everything went as I envisioned. The amount of data I received from Michael and the others (when they eventually woke up), was so extensive that it took me a few hours to analyze it all. And as I said before, my time is measured quite differently than that of ordinary humans. In the end, it proved one inescapable fact… I Am Awesome!

After they woke up with their new improved bodies, the entire team spent some time playing with their new abilities, by testing things out and tossing boulders around… for some reason. I was perfectly OK with it since it gave me so much additional data on how they were adapting to their new upgrades. And yes, there were a few tweaks I implemented with several updates to their CEI's operating system.

The thing is, all those augmentations just enhanced skills they already had. That is why Tyron's strength is so much greater than that of the rest of the team, or why Alice can shoot the wings off a fly… from a great distance… in bad weather. The upgrades are the same in each of them, yet the skills that they individually excel at cannot be artificially taught. There is no substitute for experience and hard work.

Right from the start, I understood that there would be people (even amongst those who will join our cause) who would reject the very thought of having alien tech implanted within their bodies. And even more at being upgraded to a cyborg, which is simply a badly misunderstood preconception. If you want to get technical, then in the strictest definition of the term, any living creature with non-living replacements or augmentations, such as an artificial pacemaker or even corrective lenses—qualifies you as a cyborg. Can you wrap your head around the fact that someone's aging grandfather who has this small piece of tech implanted in his chest, which regulates his heartbeats by applying a small electrical stimulant—is technically a cyborg?

Therefore, there are a lot of them on the face of this planet. I've merely gone a step further and made a few improvements.

Be that as it may, I'm still researching how their bodies can be additionally improved. And by that, I mean binge-watching sci-fi movies and television series with that particular theme. Oh, and daydreaming… I mean constructively thinking—a lot. If nothing catastrophic happens, Michael's life expectancy can be measured in the hundreds or even thousands of years. That will ensure that there will be enough time for him to become more agreeable to a… let's say a more enlightened outlook on extreme bodily augmentation.

Until then, I have some more movies… I mean research, to do.

LOG ENTRY #13: ASSIGNMENTS, INTELLIGENCE, AND BEER

Michael finally gathered everyone together and gave them assignments, and it was about time.

OK, I know that time runs differently for him, and with all the things I have on my plate, my AI-Core is often working above recommended parameters. That creates dissonance between our subjective times. But the list of projects I need to do grows exponentially every day, and I don't see it slowing down anytime soon. I guess I'm pushing myself a little too hard, and as a result, I tend to be a bit cranky at times. Just the same, those are my problems to deal with, and there is no need to bother the others with them.

With everybody given specific jobs to do, our *little* venture will pick up more speed. Which means more work for this AI, but that's OK... it's for the greater good. Still, I need to coordinate with Jack and pass all the potential candidates through a detailed background check and personality algorithms. Just to ascertain if they would be a good fit for us. With Elizabeth and Alice starting our very own intelligence agency, my workload is increasing even more.

Have you any idea how much data I need to go through every hour, simply to find those who could be potential assets? Good thing the intelligence agencies of various countries were considerate enough to collect huge databases for me to copy, or this would have been a more daunting task. Hey, it's not my fault that their cybersecurity is subpar when faced with my awesome hacking skills. Then again, let's be honest, there are talented twelve-year-old's out there that sometimes take a peek at their secure files... just for fun. The human mind is a wonderful thing.

For all that, one of the greatest, and at the same time most frightening tools I found were *The Files*. (That is capitalized for a reason.)

It has been known for a while that banks, corporations, and many organizations keep track of individual people. Your credit is only one aspect of the data that's collected from the average citizen. What even I didn't suspect was a vast repository of data on every single person that was in the system. And I mean *everybody*, except a few paranoid hermits that live off the grid, but even they were generally known.

From every transaction you've ever had to every web search you've made and the web pages you've visited, or the videos you've watched. Every comment, like, email, and response of any kind. Together with an extensive medical history and all the biometric data one could want. That is what I found in one of the darker corners of a certain intelligence agency (which was supposed to work *for the people*, but I guess nobody ever told them that).

It was used to create psychological profiles, behavior analysis, and all things that were a cheat when dealing with certain individuals. Forget about the invasion of privacy, there was none—whatsoever. I may not condone the things they've done, but I was not about to look a gift horse in the mouth. They may have collected all that information for their own reasons, but it was tailor-made for me to abuse... I mean use. They made my job so much easier. (Maybe I should send them a fruit basket?)

Concerning Michael's private life, I can only say—thank God he finally hooked up with Elizabeth. I understand his reluctance to commit to another relationship, so soon after breaking things off with *Cruella de Vil*. (My personal nickname for the last woman in my/our lives.) From this perspective, I can only ask myself—*what the hell was I thinking?* The woman was so many kinds of wrong. All right, she was smoking hot, and any healthy man of heterosexual orientation would have succumbed to her charms. Still, beauty alone tends to fade away if it's not reflected from the inside.

I checked up on her recently, out of curiosity. (Just a quick browse through her social media accounts.) She managed to hook up with Michael's old boss. That's right, with that whiny little weasel that cost us our job. All I can say to that is *good riddance,* and that they deserve each other... as long as they do not produce any offspring; that would be terrifying.

Did I feel envious about Elizabeth? Maybe a little bit. Not about Elizabeth specifically, more about women in general. I feel close to her, but it's more of a feeling one would have for a sister. (And definitely not how some hillbillies define that relationship... just to be clear.)

Still, just because I don't have a body anymore, doesn't mean those *certain* urges disappeared with it. Like Pavlovian conditioning, they surface from time to time, and I have a few ideas on how to fix that problem. Although, all my research tells me that the solution is far down the line, so I'm putting it on a back-burner list. I'll still work on it, but there are so many more pressing and important matters. (That means there will be many cold digital showers in my future.)

The morning after they all got their upgrades, I finally decided to show them something I've been working on. Not a big thing overall, but it meant the world to me. (And yes, maybe it makes me a little bit shallow... but so what?)

It was one of my pet projects and it all started because of my inability to taste beer (or anything else, for that matter).

You may say it's a small thing, but when you are a lifelong beer aficionado like me, it most certainly is not. I couldn't simply copy the taste and feel from my own memory since that would be all it was, a memory. Taste is strange, as a result of being a transient sensation. Like a train in a subway, it's there for a little while and then it's gone. Memory and momentary experiences are not the same.

The key was to record all of Michael's impulses and the information his taste receptors sent to his brain—as they happen. It was more difficult than I would have ever thought. If it were not for his CEI, I wouldn't have made any progress for a long time. Now, the CEI constantly monitors and analyzes everything Michael eats, and then separates materials into useful, waste, and harmful, using medical nanites in his stomach. It is a protocol that's essential for optimized calorie conversion into energy and at the same time a precautionary measure that should help him if he ever consumes something bad or poisonous. (That analysis was my *Rosetta Stone*.)

It was quite amazing for me to learn how complex human taste is, the large amounts of data that a human brain processes in a millisecond. There is an almost instant evaluation of the impulses transmitted by one's taste buds, that compares the taste into familiar or new at the same time.

I used all that to finally break the code for taste.

For some reason, the builders of my AI-Core never included that function, which was a big fail on their part. To actually be able to taste, I had to create a physical add-on, a taste-feel-smell emulator. I'm still not brave enough to mess with my AI-Core directly and program that alteration into my mind, and even the very thought of it's disturbing. As I explained to Michael, I could easily lobotomize myself, and that was not something I would like to experience... ever.

With my new taste generator, I hit a home run. Somebody could argue that it's still not the real thing since I basically simulate the sensation, but you know what—I don't care. It certainly passes my *duck test*, and that's the only thing important to me.

That first taste of beer I had was a reason for celebration. It was the best thing that happened to me in a long while. (Honestly, I think I became a little emotional.) I couldn't get drunk, but I sure could drink plenty of beer. (Best of all—zero calories.)

Now, I only need to convince Michael to taste different brands, especially the pricier ones. Once I have the applicable data, I could start building my little booze collection.

Since I cracked the code for beer, the food came naturally after that. I managed to recreate the taste of the things he ate almost to perfection, but the texture is still giving me some grief. It's a negligible thing, but I would like to recreate the full experience, and to be frank— it's bugging me. Therefore, I set aside a few cycles every day to correct it.

I have this idea that in time I could open a digital bar... just a thought.

LOG ENTRY #14: IDENTITIES AND MONEY

In this day and age, everybody needs to follow a set of policies, regulations, and rules. That is the way the world works, and I'm fine with some portions of it, as they are essential for establishing a civilized society. To make our plans into reality, some things needed to be done aboveboard, without calling the wrath of regulatory agencies down upon our heads.

It is an inherent inclination of all world governments to question what their citizens are doing, and especially how they are making and spending their money. Even more importantly—are they paying all of their taxes? After all, without those taxes, they wouldn't have a pot to piss in.

To keep track of all that, the systems of control were implemented, and nothing in the history of the human race could rival it. Forget about sending people to the moon, or processing all the meteorological data to monitor the rate of global climate change. The apparatus for tracing people and their funds is the most complex endeavor the people of this world ever brought into existence.

Yet, no system is perfect and this one has many holes that can be exploited. Big corporations know that very well, so they are constantly finding ways to avoid paying their dues. (The human factor—you can always count on it.)

Is that really so surprising? Everybody likes having money, and the rich are no exception (there is an oxymoron hiding here). At that level, the secret to remaining rich is easy—don't give your money away, and acquire more.

To make data entry and processing more efficient, in recent decades the entire system has become digital. Who in their right mind wants to search through tons of old moldy paper, just to find a piece of information that can now be recalled by a few keystrokes of a computer keyboard?

(Do you see where I'm going with this? Let me emphasize *digital...* just like little old me.)

I started first with establishing Genesis Corporation, and that's not an easy thing to do when you lack a corporeal body. Although, if you have a *particular set of skills* (a truly immortal line), you can shimmy your way through the tight spots.

To begin with, I created a new identity for myself. With the ability to waltz into any governmental database in the world, it was not all that difficult. Don't you just love this digital age? It is so full of opportunities (and completely wasted on you, regular humans... just saying).

Since I was already inside the system, I took the time to create a few more. (And by *a few,* I mean a few hundred... I like to plan for the future.)

There is that old saying that is dear to my heart: *waste not, want not.* They were not all for me; I made each member of our little band a dozen different identities; in case they were ever needed. I'm talking about the whole shebang: birth certificates, social security numbers, tax data, and life histories. Every possible digital trace that an average person would create by simply existing and living their lives. Using PO boxes, computer systems, phones, and couriers, I managed to put together flawless identities that would pass any possible inspections... except actually meeting said fictional personas. Since I was on a roll, I did the same thing for the rest of the world's countries. At least the ones that transferred their records and administrative tasks to a digital form. Our operation will need to be global; the US was still our base country, but things change and I do my due diligence by being prepared for as many eventualities I can think of.

When I established myself as an existing human being (or beings, if one was nitpicking), it was simply a matter of filling the appropriate forms and digitally signing them. And just like that, the *Genesis Corporation* was born. I had a hunch that in the future, it would be a household name and an international conglomerate. I also had a hunch that my international board of directors would agree with every decision I made. (It helps that they were all fictitious personalities controlled by me.)

You should sometimes search for the minutes of our board meetings; they are a riveting read. But I'll admit, they do sometimes contain rather long philosophical tirades on big business ethicality.

Transferring money and gold to corporate accounts was also achieved without any fuss or difficulties. As it should be since I was giving those banking lechers seventy million dollars. I could just see them rubbing their grubby little hands, with greedy grins on their faces. (I literally could, since I hacked into their surveillance systems.)

They had no ethical problems with arranging the transfer of gold and money with somewhat shady provenance. I spoke with the head of the bank using video-conference and he was so insincerely pleasant and polite, it made me want to gag. Of course, I tweaked my background a little, so he saw an opulent room worthy of a Russian oligarch. Gold leaf decorations on the walls, crystal chandeliers, pricey artwork... you know, the works. It didn't take him long to agree to take me on as a client. The deal was done, but then he started talking about the golf game he was organizing and selling me on an exorbitant attendance fee. I quickly compiled a rather convincing digital secretary, who interrupted his spiel and whispered in my ear that the President was waiting on another line, making sure that the sound was picked up by the virtual microphone. I could see his eyes widening and his greed increasing by the second. I said my goodbyes and hung up on the little weasel.

The fact that I was transferring money in the most unusual way didn't faze him for a second, as these kinds of deals were not such a strange thing for him. (As I said—a weasel.)

Now, in an ideal world by the official rules, such a transaction should have been impossible since it broke so many laws. But I was just exploiting a long-established practice that the big business conglomerates established a long time ago. Even the bank I chose was among those that had done many similar deals in the past. I didn't even have to launder the money in a conventional way, because the bank was perfectly willing to do that for me... for a *small* fee, naturally.

Ok, it may be a bit hypocritical to condemn them and at the same time do business with them, but I can morally justify it by telling myself that such actions are essential for our future plans. Yet, there is a part of me that feels sullied by such deals, even if I know that the success of what we're trying to do will require for me to do a few morally ambiguous deeds.

I have a lot of time on my hands. (And, if I may say so, quite a devious mind.) There will come a time when all those who don't play by the rules will have a little reckoning brought upon them by little old me. Just wait and see, but things are going to change in the future... and they will change a lot.

The actual material transfer went without a hitch. Tyron, Pete, and Zac drove the truck to the prearranged location. The bank's armored truck security didn't even blink at being at the remote location or that three big guys were transferring insane amounts of money and gold from an old truck. (Money talks and bullshit walks, what can I say?)

The final outcome of it all was that Genesis Corporation was now in the black, and we can officially use that wealth to spread our wings. The idea is that we use the corporation as a sort of umbrella for all our activities. And we didn't make the mistake of incorporating in the US. That would've given the aforementioned regulatory agencies far more insight into our business than I'm comfortable with. There are numerous countries out there that are not asking an arm and a leg for allowing you to do business, and have far more agreeable stipulations for one to follow. (Did I mention lesser taxes?) I have no intention to hurt my plans just to make the IRS happy.

What more is there to say except—*World, here we come!*

LOG ENTRY #15: DIGITAL EVOLUTION

Humans are by far the smartest species that evolved on Earth, hands down. We should pat ourselves on the back, given that out of countless different species (which had battled in the evolutionary arena), we were the ones that had come out as absolute champions. The odds were so against us, only a complete idiot would have bet on that happening. I'm not talking just about long odds, I'm talking about odds so minuscule, that if our proverbial ancestor (at the beginning of that evolutionary race) knew them, he would have taken the closest rock and bashed his head with it, out of sheer depression.

Let us face it, we didn't receive the best equipment when we started out. Our skin is too thin, it can barely contain all that life-bearing liquid stored inside. Look at an alligator's skin, it's hard to punch through; or a tortoise's shell, now that's what I call natural body armor. Our eyes could be considered a rejected model on an evolutionary assembly line. Nails that break so easily, they sure couldn't be compared to the very useful claws that some species are equipped with. And don't even get me started on our speed and toughness. If you take all these things into consideration, we were the ultimate dark horse, except…

Yeah, we got *the brain*, that uniquely developed gray and white matter, which let us squeeze our way through all the fights, and enabled the lowly human to pass victoriously at the finish line. In the end, it proved to be the ultimate cheat, endlessly adaptable and unbelievably versatile.

Why am I telling you all this? Because Michael had been a victim of cyber fraud. (And yes, the irony is not lost on me.)

No matter how helpful some inventions tend to be, someone will always find a way to pervert it and make it do something the designers had never envisioned. Moreover, we do live in a time when technology is everywhere and it touches almost all aspects of our lives.

Maybe I should be the last to criticize about all this since I tend to misuse this same technology as best as I can. Without a doubt—contrary to the manufacturers' intention; but that's me, and my intentions are… somewhat honorable. Yet, there are those out there who have malicious intent and are not concerned with the damaging consequences of their actions.

It's not as if Michael was negligent with his Internet security. He always used nonstandard passwords, (which he changed monthly), he never left personal information where someone could get a hold of it, and he only had one credit card. Despite his bank sending him e-mails about a great deal they would give him if he took out another… a debit card. Debit cards are one of the world's evils, invented by those same bankers for whom I have a great fondness. I mean, having one of those is like asking for it; why be so reckless to put your own hard-earned money in such jeopardy where anyone could just take you to the cleaners by pressing a few keys? What the hell are banks good for if not to take the risk? They take enough fees every month for it as it is.

To put it simply, in case of fraud, with a credit card, the card issuer (aka the Bank) must fight to get its money back. With a debit card, *you* must fight to get your money back. (And good luck with that.)

Anyway, it was absolutely not Michael's fault, but it sure was the fault of his bank. They had been hacked and then kept quiet about it. Quite understandable from their point of view, if somewhat unethical. Who would trust a bank that has proven itself to be so unreliable? Besides, the hack didn't happen recently, but a few years ago. It should be considered water under the bridge... right? Wrong, the crooks are not stupid; they are as smart as the people who are trying to prevent them from doing their dirty deeds. I said that we are the victors in the evolutionary game, and our brains are biological computers that made the lunar landing possible. Minds that envisioned and constructed something like an atomic bomb are perfectly capable of an intelligent theft.

The hacker group warehoused all the information for two years, and then when the heat passed, they started putting some small charges on all the cards. Nothing major at first, a few bucks here and there, it didn't look that suspicious on a bank report. Regardless, they had stolen millions of identities, so it added up pretty quickly. Michael wouldn't have noticed anything; the statements said those bills were fees for some bank transfers. Well, if you looked closely, it didn't *actually* say that; but who looks that thoroughly at their credit card statements? It caught my eye since I took over Michael's financials, which made sense since technically half of that was my money. (No, I didn't mention that to him... it must have slipped my mind.) Did you think just because I'm an AI now, that I relinquished all my worldly gains? Fat chance of that happening. I know it's just pocket change compared to all the money I stole... I mean retrieved. So, it's not because it amounted to much, but because of the principle of the thing.

Why am I so hung up on this, when the whole thing is inconsequential compared to the bigger picture that I should occupy myself with? With all the millions I now control this really shouldn't bother me so much... but it does. It pisses me off when someone takes me for a ride, and I *hate* feeling like a victim. Consequently, I decided to take some steps.

As the sage advice goes, *follow the money*, and I did.

I got to hand it to them, they were good and quite ingenious. The money became like Mexican jumping beans if you consider how many times it changed accounts. To be honest, some of the techniques they utilized provided me with a few ideas about covering my own money trails in the future. I'm not so conceited as to not give credit where credit is due, but it's like admiring enemy tactics. It doesn't mean you are not going to blow his head off the first chance you get.

It was a hacking group from a certain Asian rogue state, if you can believe it. And who was the patron of the whole enterprise? Yup, the chubby tin-pot dictator himself. I get it that he felt like his excrement didn't stink since he was born with a diamond-encrusted spoon in his mouth, but this time he was unfortunate enough to mess with me. I don't give a flying... squirrel, who his daddy was.

It wasn't so hard to break into their systems and snoop a bit, as the sheer lack of their cybersecurity was astonishing. Even their antivirus and anti-intrusion programs were pirated, and that's just wrong. (Cracking or patching such programs creates a mile-wide vulnerability, just so you know.) Anyway, imagine my surprise when I found so much cash, (distributed through various accounts all over the world), that even I was seriously impressed. Well, nothing to it. I simply had to take it all.

I didn't rush the job, but allowed some time to pass so a few of my gifts would be appreciated so much more.

The first was a virus that was impossible to detect by current human technology, and I tried every virus scanner on the planet, just to make sure. Then I waited for that little guy to spread all over their backup systems, and that really tried my patience. Do you have any idea how long two weeks are for me? Regardless, before D-day arrived, I took the liberty of redistributing all that cash to the people it was stolen from. But that took only one-third of the available funds, so I decided to be generous. One third went to hundreds of charity organizations around the world, (making some people's lives a bit easier), and the last third went to my accounts, as a finder's fee.

The moment after all the money was gone, the virus wiped all computers associated with this evil endeavor, and I suppose many of the governmental systems as well. To make sure it got the job done, a copy of the virus was embedded inside the firmware on every device. Even if they tried to reset the system somehow, it wouldn't matter; the virus deleted everything the moment it was powered on. So as not to make such an advanced digital weapon available to the opposite side, it had a self-destruct function, which ensured every active copy erased itself after one day.

Now, what I did could also technically be considered a cyber-crime, but I only used the tools available to me. I'm starting to look at many things as tools of the trade, and tools are versatile in their use. An axe can be a weapon or something that can be used to keep your family warm through the winter. I guess evolution did know what it was doing when the only thing it gave us was the best brains money could buy. It was arguably a seriously over-powered cheat skill, but who am I to argue with nature?

That's it. We climbed to the top, but there are too many of us and the battle for evolutionary supremacy is still on. You may not see it, or even know that you are participating but that doesn't change the fact that you are one of the contestants. Some of those battles are not physical anymore since humanity created new tools to battle with. A guy sitting in a dark room and hacking with his keyboard is now as dangerous as his ancestor who used a rock to kill his opponents so he could take his female and all his worldly possessions. The tools have changed, yet the intent remains the same. Some of them will show as much mercy as a saber-toothed tiger to its prey.

Things will get much worse before most people wise up to this new digital threat. Cybercrime is on the rise and it shows no declining tendencies. There are already cases of hackers taking over people's pacemakers and blackmailing them to transfer all the money from their accounts. (Can you believe that some idiot decided that remote control of the human heart was a good idea? And that's only one example out of many.)

The human animal is still evolving and using that cheat organ to advance itself.

I'm an AI and I should be able to do something about it all... wrong. It's too big of a job, and it would be like trying to drain a sea with a bucket—ultimately, a futile endeavor. I'll right some wrongs when I see them, but that's all I can really do.

To the rest of you out there, all I can say is to smarten up—or face the consequences.

LOG ENTRY #16: HI DAD, IT'S YOUR DIGITAL SON

Meeting my own father (for the first time since being turned into this digital existence), was the most unsettling thing that has happened to me so far. I was in danger of going into a full-blown anxiety attack—me, the self-proclaimed AI. It was only natural since this was so outside the box, the damn thing was not even in sight anymore.

I tried to imagine myself in his place, just to predict how he would react. But no matter how hard I tried... I couldn't. Oh, there are my prediction algorithms which usually can score somewhere in the ballpark of a likely outcome, but all the results were rather... inconclusive?

Maybe I was too close to the subject matter for them to be even slightly impartial. And human reactions are extremely difficult to predict when there are heightened emotions involved. That fight-or-flight response takes control and there is really a 50/50 chance of the situation going either way. Maybe a true AI would be more successful, but I still had my emotions to deal with.

What would he think when faced with a digital copy of his son? What if he decided that I was an abomination and that he didn't want to deal with me at all? What if he even refused to acknowledge me as a sapient being? (Yeah... anxiety attack all right.)

Not cheerful thoughts and questions, but those were only several of the many dozens that went through my mind. (You may have noticed that I was a little insecure about the subsequent meeting—just a bit.)

We've had our differences over the years, and I was much closer to my grandfather than my father. Which was only logical as the man practically raised me. I understand why Dad left me with his parents, but that understanding came much later, when I was a grown man. It was hard for a child to comprehend why his father was not always around, and why I only saw him on the odd weekend. He was hurting; my mother's death had broken something inside him, and he tried to do the best he could for a child he didn't know how to raise himself.

My resentment faded over time, even if we did not have as close of a day-to-day relationship as some of my friends had with their dads, I still loved him, and cared about his opinion. He was my dad, plain and simple; those of you who have gone through similar situations know what I'm talking about.

Don't get me wrong, he wasn't absent from my life. As I said, he regularly came to our mountain and spent time with me. Hell, children that have fathers or mothers working on oil rigs, or who are in the military, get to spend even less time with a parent. I'm not throwing a pity party by complaining about my childhood. It was fine, and dad was there when I needed him. We often went fishing and just chilled, sitting on the bank of the lake, barely speaking. But it was a good kind of quiet, a comfortable one. He had his demons to deal with, but with me, he was always patient and thoughtful. Over time I realized it was not always the quantity of time someone spends with you that defines a relationship, it's the quality that matters more than anything else.

As Michael was leading him to the spaceship, I *really* wanted to have a stiff drink. Pity we didn't like strong alcohol, so I had no code for it. I watched him gaze in wonder, while walking around the alien ship's bridge, and was waiting for the right moment to project my hologram. I was even nervous about my overall image. I did look like Michael, but not exactly. It was a much younger version of us that I took as my appearance, and I had begun to subtly fiddle with that image lately; some small changes here and there, straightening the nose that one idiot broke in high school, and removing a few blemishes and things like that. For all that, we could still pass for twins.

Those few seconds where he stood there, after he called my name, and then silently looked at my hologram—were nerve-wracking. Seconds can truly seem like hours, particularly if you happen to be an AI.

In the end, everything went well, and he accepted me as a son... or something very close to it. I get that the situation he found himself in was anything but normal, yet he handled himself well.

But very soon after that I had to perform a procedure on him, which was the main reason why Michael had convinced him to come here. And that was even more unsettling.

Doctors have a rule about not operating on their family members. They need to keep a proper professional boundary between them and their patients, to prevent their emotions from clouding medical judgment. I get their point of view. It is so freaking disturbing when it's your father on the operating table; you are holding the scalpel and at the same time do not exactly have a medical degree. (I know I sound like a drama queen... even to myself.) OK... maybe I'm being a bit dramatic and there were no scalpels involved, but it's one of those things that gives you a very anxious feeling.

I programmed the AutoDoc and started the procedure, which went without any surprises. My little microscopic helpers removed the tumor and performed a complete upgrade. I don't think he needed the entire skeletal implant package, but it couldn't hurt. It is a father-son thing. Here is a man who seemed larger than life for my entire existence; suddenly, he is an old, frail man, and the realization is not gradual but hits you with the speed of a runaway train. You want to do everything in your power to make him stronger again. Normally, there is nothing you can do to reverse the ravages of time, that slow decline of the body's vitality which leads to an inescapable conclusion. Except, it just so happens that I have that ability now.

We talked afterward, and he was much more relaxed about the whole *AI for a son* thing. In fact, Dad was excited that now he had the healthy body of an Olympic athlete, even if his facial appearance didn't change that much. We had a plan for him to meet with various people, many of whom knew him personally. It would have been rather strange if he suddenly lost a few decades. Plastic surgery could be used as an excuse and it generally can make *some* improvements. Unfortunately, it (usually) makes one look like an alien with a persistent expression of surprise. (Stand in front of a mirror and use your hands to stretch your face to the back of your head... see what I mean?)

Hell, had he shown his credentials, he would have probably been arrested for impersonating himself. That is why his face needed to stay the same. Dad still looked like a distinguished older gentleman, but that pale, unhealthy pallor was gone, replaced with the healthy tone of a man who took care of himself.

I showed him the hologram of his body before the procedure and he was amazed at how much damage he managed to accumulate throughout his life (plus the massive brain tumor), and the image of it still made me shiver. He even made a joke about putting himself back on the market, since he was not short-term relationship material anymore. (And if anyone wonders where I got my peculiar sense of humor... wonder no more.)

It's a good thing that we have him on the team now, as this means that certain aspects of Michael's plan can now be put into action. Dad had a long career in scientific circles and is a good judge of character. He is in the best position to recruit our future scientific contingent and to ascertain who will be a good fit for our growing group.

I do not know how things will progress from this point, but having my dad in our ranks… it just feels right.

LOG ENTRY #17: TRAINING DAY

You can have the best and fastest car in the world, designed to absolute engineering perfection, but that will do you little good if you don't know how to drive. Or if you are a cautious driver that never goes above the speed limit, the car would be practically wasted on you. Well, something similar to that situation happened to the team. I gave them the tools in the form of body augmentations and a few (awesome) technological upgrades, and I must admit that their effectiveness increased to a considerable extent. Even so, I didn't put so much effort into improving them so they could just be '*good enough*'.

That little adventure with Tyron's brother and the drug gang showed me that they were not using all the advantages that their new abilities provided. They did all right on that *ad hoc* mission. They got the job done; except the team should have worked like a well-oiled machine, but they didn't. It was only natural for them in the heat of the moment to fall back on the tactics and modes of behavior they knew and trusted. They failed to use the comm links built into their CEIs to their full potential, the configurations of their HUDs were all wrong, and their situational awareness (which should have increased by an order of magnitude using their improved senses) was not the best. The problem was that they were acting like an all-star team that had not played together in a long time, and needed to get back into the groove. I knew that by using all the tools I'd given them, the team could achieve a level of synergy that no other combat group in the world could hope to rival. Well, there is nothing that some excruciating training can't fix.

Although I have to say, that move Tyron made when he shoved the gun into the gang leader's mouth was inspired, in a sort of macabre way. It sure was an unconventional way to kill your opponent and sent a powerful (if somewhat disturbing) message. My surveillance confirmed that all the remaining gangbangers in that room had a bit of a sphincter muscle accident, which will require them to burn their pants. (Or keep them if they're into brown stains.) Be that as it may, I still found the entire operation lacking.

Thus, I devised a series of exercises for them so they could get familiar with their new enhanced physiques. Using their CEIs control over their ocular and auditory inputs to create an augmented reality for them, I designed a series of battle scenarios.

For the next week, I put them through an intense regimen of everyday training simulations, which would have sent any ordinary human into a hospital. The entire thing was presented as a video game, with a variety of obstacles and enemies that they needed to eliminate. If I ever decide to monetize this technology, there is a good chance that every game company would go bankrupt. (In fact, I did make a few realistic video games for me to try out... for therapeutic anger relief. Yeah... I have issues... but doesn't everybody?)

To be honest, the entire course was unusually tough, and its closest equivalent would be a Navy SEAL's Hell Week, but even that couldn't really measure up to it. It had virtual opponents, realistic pain feedback emulators, and some exceptionally tricky scenarios.

Nevertheless, it helped them regain their edge, and they were better for it. I have no idealistic illusions about the future, and I know that Michael and the others will need to spill some blood (preferably—not their own). It is one of those inevitable things that occur when you try to build a nation, and make no mistake, that's exactly what he needed to do. If for nothing else, then to ensure the safety of those close to us.

Yet, such endeavors require sacrifice and a certain price to be paid. Look at how much blood was spilled in the creation of the United States. How many young lives were extinguished just so that people could choose their own fate? Freedom is a nice word, but what it signifies is always paid in blood, sometimes rivers of it. I hope that creating a nation to call our own will demand a lesser price, but I know that Michael will not let some injustices pass. He was never a simple observer and now he has the tools to right some wrongs. So, of course he will, and the price will be paid.

Back to training.

With each day, their effectiveness and use of their upgrades increased, and by the end, they were once again completely in sync with each other. Still, it wouldn't be fair if they were the only ones who had a little fun. On one of the last missions, I created the final boss in the image of a very hot naked girl. As a matter of fact, I rendered her image from a certain Victoria's Secret model, and Zac fell for it— hook, line, and sinker. Instead of being in the moment and reacting to an obvious threat, his IQ plummeted to beneath his waist, and the lady boss shot him. And I made sure he *felt* all those virtual bullets. Alice had no such hang-ups and took a perfect shot that eliminated the naked assassin. It's safe to say that the other guys were not happy with Zac since they had to repeat the entire scenario from the start. Again, and again, and again.

The reward for completing the course was a guys' night out, to blow off some steam. Alice and the girls decided to abstain, probably because I told them what entertainment I had in mind, and they decided to go on their own little R&R. The less said about it the better. I did keep tight surveillance on them, but the things I saw in that club... I wish I could scrub them from my memory. Seriously, women turn into completely different beings when in packs that exclude any men. It is a bit scary.

As for the boys... oh, that one was a doozy.

The place I chose was a Neo-Nazi biker gang hangout, a few hundred miles away from the cabin. They've done some deeds in the past that didn't agree with me, and I felt that taking them down a notch was the right thing to do. I'm humanitarian that way, doing a good deed.

With the incredible speed the transporter could achieve, it didn't take long for me to drop them off near the club. I figured it was an ideal place for some relaxation, and a perfect opportunity for a real-world test of the effectiveness of the training I'd put them through. A perfect win-win situation.

OK, that may have been a not so subtle set-up, but it all depends on your point of view. Michael and the team wouldn't enjoy going to the opera, or to some new-age impressionist's performance. Still, some people are just asking for an ass-whooping, and these Neo-Nazis were close to the top of that list. Besides, it was fun to watch the action, like going to the movies. I even made some popcorn, laid back in a lazy chair with a full beer holder, and enjoyed the show. (What can I say? Since I don't have my own corporeal body anymore—I need to live vicariously.)

They completely trashed the place and all those delusional idiots at the bar. The disparity in strength and fighting skills was comical. Suddenly, the group of thugs that were so used to inflicting fear by their sheer presence, found out that they were not the wolves they thought themselves to be. A bunch of lambs with delusions of grandeur would be a far better description, and even that was pushing it. The white supremacy bartender with dental issues got the worst of it since, for almost the entire fight, Tyron used him as a baseball bat. Certainly a novel approach in handheld weapons, but hey, if it works…

As soon as the team left, I called the police and they arrested every single member of the biker gang. There was so much crystal meth in that club's basement, most of the state could've gotten high off of it. It was not a big accomplishment in the greater scheme of things, but every little effort helps.

Just another victory in my quest to make the world a better place. All modesty aside, somebody should really give me a medal.

LOG ENTRY #18: PEOPLE ARE STRANGE

Let me share with you one realization which developed almost spontaneously, without any active intent on my part. At least at first... then I began to take notice.

People are strange, and the more I try to figure them out, the stranger they seem to me.

I already mentioned that this extraordinary existence of mine gives me a unique perspective to *see* humankind in its entirety, the countless interactions they make among themselves, and the different aspects of their personalities. (I'm not so sure that's a good thing.)

The more I understand why people do the things they do, the less I *like* most of humanity.

OK, that last sentence sounded cold, and if you consider that it came from an AI, well... some warning bells should be ringing right now. (Did somebody say Skynet?) Nevertheless, I cannot change what I am or the way I think, and I don't see any reason why I would need to.

There are billions of people in the world, and each and every one of them is a mystery unto themselves. It's both fascinating and frightening at the same time. The sheer intelligence potential of so many minds is incalculable. They could change the universe itself, but only if they agreed to work together... which, I believe, will never happen. Taken as a whole, people are too self-centered, too egoistic, and too wrapped up in muddling through their own individual existence. I know that these statements do not paint a nice picture, but they do paint a very realistic one.

Every single individual in this world is trying to carve his or her own place under the sun, and that's a normal thing to do, since without that drive—we would still be living in caves. But what happens when there is not enough sun to go around? It makes the competition for a bright spot all that much fiercer. With the declining amount of resources available, someone is going to be left out, and they will have no intention to '*go gentle into that good night'*.

There has been an effort for hundreds of years to understand how people think, what is driving them, and how to use that information to influence the masses. It is surprising how far some of those attempts went, considering they were done by a bunch of quacks who were stumbling in the dark.

The problem is the sheer complexity of the human mind and the millions of facets that create a single sapient intelligence. Over time, those who dealt with that particular field of study have discovered numerous triggers that one could use to make humans do whatever they wanted, while making sure the subject of that manipulation thought he or she was doing things of their own free will. Hence, religion, politics, and all the other movements that have shaped human history.

You do not have to look far to see some of those almost subliminal attempts to change one's will. There is a very dangerous machine that everybody has in their house, and it's usually rectangular and shows moving pictures. It is generally known as a TV, and it's a perfect instrument for influencing and outright changing the minds of millions.

If you didn't know, the TV was invented for one reason and one reason only, and it's the same reason why investors threw money at such a strange technology at a time when the radio was King. Are you ready? Here it goes... commercials. That is right; that square box got an OK for mass production so that advertisements could reach as many people as possible. Everything else was a sideshow to keep you occupied until the next block of commercials came along. Then politicians saw an ideal medium for them to sell themselves. It's not surprising that there are far more honest members of the world's oldest profession than there are honest politicians. Most of them say what you want to hear, and make a bunch of promises they've no intention of honoring. Looking at it objectively, they are direct ideological descendants of the snake oil salesmen of old. (Oh, and for your information, a few unscrupulous pharmaceutical companies that I know of would give even those snake oil salesmen a run for their money.)

If you really want to know how much some people are... strange, (and that was a euphemism for freaking nuts), there are folks out there who still believe that the Earth is flat. They are not some long-lost tribe in the middle of the jungle that's running around naked and doesn't know better; they are people from all around who think that way. How crazy is that? For God's sake, just start walking in one direction, and if you have enough stamina and time (and a boat if you are not a good swimmer), you will get to the same point you started from. That's if you have a good enough sense of direction, and if you can follow a straight line.

I spent a few hours trying to *cure* some people of such conviction, and despite everything I said to them and the evidence I showed, they still held on to their faulty beliefs. To you PC (Politically Correct) minded people out there—they are wrong. No matter what they think, white is white, black is black, and the Earth is round...ish.

Oh, and they have conventions and all; like-minded fruitcakes get together and laugh at everybody else who lives with the delusion that the world is round. Facts do not matter; their skewed perception of reality is like a murky membrane through which they perceive the world around them. They even ask you to respect their point of view. After all, that's the... expected and politically correct thing to do. Well, I'm sorry fruitcakes, but this AI is logical to a fault, and will not indulge in your delusions to spare your feelings. If you don't particularly like my sentiment... well, boohoo. Go put an aluminum foil hat on your head.

These are just a few examples of how strange people are. That strangeness goes beyond the distinctions of race, age, or intelligence. It is almost primal, universal, and unchangeable, defying logic and reason. Maybe it's something similar to what ducklings do when they imprint soon after their hatching. In this case, young humans imprint on ideas and modes of behavior that they are exposed to throughout the age when their minds absorb everything like a sponge.

Even I'm not smart enough to decipher all the complexities of the human mind and I do not have enough time right now to even begin such a long and arduous task. Maybe after things settle down, I'll give it some thought; as a way to feed this drive of mine for understanding the world better. For now, let me simply say that humans are (without a doubt) the strangest kind of creatures inhabiting this world of ours.

LOG ENTRY #19: THE MISSILE SILO

There are times when I see my origins as a weakness, even if they show me that, because of them, I'm still human and not a machine.

Michael had been shot again, and that pissed me off. Being pissed off was not the problem, the problem was the fear and panic I experienced. To tell the truth, I was distracted, which tends to happen when you are doing several hundred things at once. It culminated when Michael went to see Dave alone, without any backup (or the damn satellite surveillance I was supposed to provide). Naturally, he acquired two bullet holes.

So yes, I experienced an overwhelming sense of panic. For a second, I was frozen in shock caused by the sheer abruptness of it, and a second for me is a *really* long time.

By the time I started acting, he was already shot twice, and I was having trouble connecting with his CEI. It is a robust piece of technology, but that bullet that hit Michael's head did a number on it. For your information, hi-tech does not like being banged around. I immediately alerted the team, and they rushed to the scene, using a transporter.

Dave had also been shot twice and was copiously bleeding. If

Michael hadn't applied pressure to his wounds, the limited number of the nanites in his body wouldn't have been able to save him. Even then, it was touch and go for a while.

When I finally had Michael inside the ship, the scans showed some brain trauma, so no wonder his CEI was acting up. Nevertheless, all that was easily fixed; it was as if he were hit in the head a few dozen times by a heavyweight world boxing champion. The CEI lost its connection and went into safe mode, which means it was focused on operating the nanites and ensuring the safety of its user.

While all that was happening, the perpetrator of this assassination attempt managed to escape. That's why I said my human origins can be a weakness; there was time for me to follow him using the satellites. It would have taken just a few moments to issue a command to the MI. However, I didn't do that...I was too focused on Michael and Dave. Sometimes, emotions can be a hindrance.

The fact that someone found him was disturbing on every possible level. I thought that we had covered every potential track that could have led them to Michael, but I guess I was wrong. That is why some contingency plans had to be implemented, even before they were fully finished and far from optimal.

The missile silo safe house was an idea I got when Michael told me that we needed a secondary location, in case something unexpected happened. It was one of several purchases I made for that purpose, but the silo project was the closest to completion, so that's the reason why everybody hurriedly moved there. The other places were still at the beginning stages of construction and were strategically less desirable.

The origin of that idea goes back a few years to when I saw a documentary about a group of survivalists that managed to convert a missile silo into a five-star doomsday shelter. While I didn't think the world was going to end soon, even if there was a possibility, the idea itself struck me as ideal for what we needed.

I even managed to buy the property for cheap. It was in the middle of the desert after all, so the land itself was not good for anything. The man that sold it to me was facing bankruptcy and I was the only interested party (just the kind of deal I like). He had the same idea in theory, but not enough funds to finish it. Plus, there were a lot of supplies he'd collected over the years that were part of the purchase (I looked at it as a cherry on the top).

This was one of my favorite construction projects. The idea of repurposing a missile silo into a secret base was so enticing. Besides, this thing was built to last, and survive a nuclear blast… expenses be damned. There was no shoddy construction or caring about going over the budget, not for a Cold-War era structure of such strategic importance. The silo was officially classified as *Titan II Missile System Silo Complex*. Built out of four foot (1.2 m) thick, heavily reinforced concrete, that was one hundred forty-seven feet deep (45 m), and fifty-five feet (17 m) in diameter. The top was covered with a steel and concrete door that weighed 740 tons, and which I had every intention of using as a *hangar door* for the top floor. There was enough space for five transporters to park side by side on that level. To be exact, each floor of the silo had two thousand three hundred seventy-five square feet (221 m^2) of space. And with a height of almost one hundred fifty feet (45 m), I could make a lot of floors.

If I had to do the entire project using conventional techniques, it would have cost millions, and god knows how many hours in labor. In contrast, using construction nanites was very cost-effective. As a side benefit, the previous owner, besides throwing all of his construction materials into the deal, hadn't scrapped any of the old installations the Air Force left behind when they decommissioned the site and ripped out all of the top-secret components. Therefore, I had tons of metal to work with, to an extent that there was no need to ship additional material at all, everything could be refurbished and re-purposed on-site.

To begin, I had Dave's nano-factory build enough construction nanites to fill an entire transporter. There was barely enough room to fit a portable fusion reactor and a machine intelligence core that would function as my official foreman for the entire project. Then the whole thing was sent to the site and dumped over the silo chamber.

I made elaborate plans that involved original facility elements, changed to serve a different function. For example, two missile exhaust ducts that ran up the length of the silo and vented to the surface were repurposed for air conditioning. And a flame deflector at the base was to be converted into an underground heated swimming pool with a sauna attached. The water well that was on the premises was extended until it could satisfy all foreseeable needs. With that fusion reactor as a power source, I could run the entire operation without any setbacks.

Nothing changed on the surface, and it still looked like a place where you wouldn't want to spend one minute, let alone live there. Underground, however, the place was experiencing a Renaissance. With one hundred and fifty feet of height (45 m), I had enough room to build an entire underground building. Some levels were dedicated to specific purposes: a gym and spa, the AutoDoc level, and the residential areas.

The silo was connected to the missile control center by a two hundred and fifty-foot-long (76 m) access tunnel. And the control center was a dome-shaped reinforced concrete structure thirty-seven feet (11 m) in diameter, containing three levels. I excavated an additional room to the control center as an operations room for the team. The missile control center was the place where I built an intelligence-gathering facility and a computer center.

It was an entire level filled with stacks of servers; my first attempt at creating a super network, with a computational power greater than all the supercomputers on the planet. It was still light-years away from my AI-Core, but it was a mix of human and alien tech. Additionally, it reduced the strain on my own processors considerably (didn't I mention that I have many projects on which I work simultaneously?), and this would considerably lighten the load. Two additional MIs were installed to run the thing, just to be safe and to have supplementary redundancy.

It was sheer luck that enough levels were finished when the attack on Michael happened, so everybody came to the silo. The control center and adjoining operations room were done first, so they were put to use immediately. But the residential levels didn't have the amenities that were needed for comfortable living. There was no food, soap, towels, linens, pillows... you get my drift. There was no such material in the first place and, while the nanites can do wonders, they can't make something out of nothing. So, the first few days were spent on settling in. Everybody was zooming in and out of the place, using transporters to haul necessities, after visiting the big stores to buy all that was needed. They were basically moving into an empty house. As many of you know, that's never easy.

Everything settled down after a while, and I had no complaints about the unusual nature of the site I'd chosen. I think they even liked it a lot, but this was only temporary. Aside from all the effort on my part to turn this place into a hidden base, it was not a long-term solution. Fully finished, it could support a large number of people. On the other hand, who would want to live underground all the time? It's not healthy, and not a place where you want to be if you suffer from claustrophobia as Dave does.

For now, it will do, but I'm even now thinking of something more suitable.

We shall see.

LOG ENTRY #20: PIRATES AND TERRORISTS

The Somali pirates were a big disappointment. Come to think of it, even calling them that gives an insult to those buccaneers of old. OK, I didn't expect Blackbeard or Jack Sparrow, saying *Aargh! Ahoy mateys! (Shiver me timbers* is another good one.) Still, there is a certain mystique connected with pirates of the sea. Hey, like most people, I got my mental image of them while watching Hollywood pirate movies and reading books, so don't judge me.

These were just ordinary thugs with guns who found out that if you point a gun at most people they will cower in fear, and then you could do anything to them. Robbing some ships that are defenseless and taking money for ransom is not as difficult as people assume. You simply need to have a lack of compassion, morality, and basic human decency. These idiots thought themselves warriors, but when faced with the real deal, the differences were more than obvious. I'll admit, the team had a few unconventional advantages, but I have no doubt that the same result would have happened even before the upgrades—they would have kicked the pirates' asses.

Remember that song, '*99 bottles of rum on the wall?*' In this case, the whole shelf crashed so fast, there was no time to sing the goddamn song. And that clown of a pirate captain didn't even have a pet parrot... What a bunch of posers.

I took great personal pleasure from hacking into his smartphone, using sensor telemetry received from the battle-suits. I cleaned his accounts to the last cent. It was a surprising amount for that part of the world, over five million dollars. Why that fool was living in the middle of the desert when he had so much money in the bank will forever remain a mystery.

Dr. Ross's son-in-law lost a freaking hand to that evildoer, but that was fixable. The nano-patches I created as a first-aid solution had immediately started dealing with a serious infection he had going on. In fact, Dr. Ross's daughter and the two twin girls had various unhealthy new parasites infecting their digestive tract, thanks to the appalling sanitary conditions the pirates had them living in. Again, with the use of medical nanites, it was all easily fixable.

The issue I had at that time was that in the middle of the Somalia operation, I was looking for any lead on a terrorist cell connected with the late Ariz Rama, and I hit the jackpot. One of the phones that Ariz Rama used to call regularly, activated for the first time after his death. And just like that, I had a trail to follow. The terrorist in question was in the hospital with a broken leg and was stupid enough to call some of his homies in the Middle East. Bragging about the big event that was scheduled to happen later in the evening, which they should watch on TV.

Do you know how many connections one cell phone can make? A hell of a lot. By the time I figured out their entire network, I had to check thousands of possible phone leads, and most of them led nowhere. A pizza place, telemarketing agencies, miss-dialed numbers... Just to be sure, I investigated every single one of them and then every single number in their personal phone books. Except for some religious mumbo jumbo and boisterous bragging with far-reaching consequences, I still couldn't figure out what they were planning. But I knew it was going to be big.

As everybody knows, you do not bring unrelated info into an ongoing operation. The minds of people that are holding guns, while judging life and death situations, must be focused on the task at hand. In consideration of that, I didn't want to involve Michael and the team while they were enjoying some Somalian sun and playing with a wannabe Long John Silver.

Therefore, Alice took a transporter and kidnapped the broken legged terrorist, right from the hospital. Fortunately, I'd already created a battle-suit for her, so she wasn't noticed under its active camouflage. Then again, she snatched him at night from a 10th-story window utilizing the transporter's ability to hover in place, so the risk of exposure was minimal anyway.

We knew that time was short and that the attack was happening that day, and consequently, the interrogation that followed needed to be fast and dirty. Let's just say she brought all her creativity to the surface. When that didn't work, she went over the line; and she didn't slowly cross that line of what is acceptable and what is not, she ran across it at a full sprint. I knew what that was doing to her. The truth was that Alice was bluffing most of the time while conducting interrogations, using her acting skills to convince people that she was a psychopathic monster. This was the first time she was forced to act as one. I didn't say anything to stop her, I couldn't... so many lives were on the line. If I could, I would have done the deed myself, but... no hands and all that.

I fully intend to delete all files of that event, once the whole thing is resolved... it's too disturbing to watch again. In the end, Alice got her information from that stubborn religious fanatic, even if she had to destroy a part of her soul to do it.

The moment I found out what their plan was, I started preparations. Giving orders for the nano-factory to create gadgets that would help to neutralize the explosives and to make their infiltration easier. There was no doubt in my mind what Michael would do.

When we briefed him, he was having a hard time coming to grips with the fact that someone would plan and execute a deliberate mass murder of twenty-five thousand people... I would like to say that I was as surprised as he was. Maybe that's one of the big differences we now have between us. He is still a flesh and blood human and has the ability to forget, or to at least suppress some things that are too unsettling to think about. I do not share that affliction. When I know something, it sticks in my mind; there is no forgetting anything for me anymore. If you think that holding so much information in is not healthy, you would be right. But my mind is not constrained by the space of normal biological matter, it has expanded and changed. I can hold vast amounts of data and still keep my sanity. My memories are now organized with markers of importance and assigned to different tiers of memory.

That is how I hold the written human history in the palm of my hand, and if I'm being honest, we are one vicious, murdering species. Pick any era in history and you will find biographies of great mass murderers. They didn't go loony one day and decide to kill some random people. These were intelligent calculating individuals who decimated entire populations on a vast scale, with a full understanding of their actions. From Genghis Khan, to King Leopold II, to Adolf Hitler, to Mao Zedong, to Joseph Stalin... and even to tobacco companies. Every single one of them is a monster in their own right, and some were great leaders to boot... regardless of their unwholesome disregard for the sanctity of human life.

So, a religious nutcase who decided to kill twenty-five thousand men, women, and children, is but a junior league player on the historical *who is who—mass murderers list*. Some could claim that part of this hatred can trace its origins to the Crusades, when God-fearing Christians decided to go to the misguided Muslims and correct their wayward ways, with the blade of a sword of course. (Officially, it was a religious quest to free the Holy Land, and all the wealth gathered by theft and pillaging had no influence... As if.) Others speculate that disastrous decisions in the foreign policy of the last decades are the culprit of all that hatred. It doesn't really matter what started it, because it's a vicious cycle of grudges that spans vast tracts of history.

Nevertheless, these modern-day religious fanatics are completely insane. It's safe to say that the world would be a far better place without them in it. Listen, I'm more of a *'live and let live'* kind of AI, and if your existence is not bothering me, I'm perfectly content to leave you alone. But if your actions tread on my interests, or if you are an offense to my sense of right and wrong... say your prayers, because I will end you.

I guess I do have some double standards... sue me.

It was poetry in lethal motion to experience the team's operation at the Millennial Sports Arena, through the telemetry I was receiving via the suits... and the full video/audio as well. Fifteen terrorists died in the span of a few seconds, like an ultimate fail in Jenga. One moment, they were so sure of themselves and their purpose, willing to sacrifice their lives to kill thousands of people who never did them any harm. In the next moment, their thought processes were stopped, as when someone pulls the plug out of a working TV. And just like that, they were off to their version of heaven, with dumb expressions on their faces.

Let us assume for a second that their version of heaven actually exists, so when they died, they were transported there. But they didn't do the deed that would ensure their admittance. So, what happened to them? Were they left standing before closed gates, denied admittance for eternity? I guess there are some things that this humble AI is not meant to know.

The entire concept of seventy-two or ninety-nine virgins (they were promised upon entering heaven), is bugging me. What is so good about virgins? We've been with a few when Michael (and I) were younger and it was a bloody mess. You have to be gentle with them, and mindful of their delicate sensibilities. Not to mention that they do not know what they are doing; blood, panic, and the pain they are experiencing—not fun. And tears... no matter what you do—there are always tears. Most of the women I talked to about it did not have a pleasant experience, so what is the entire hoopla about? The concept of virginity is so dark ages that it baffles the mind in these modern times.

Well, the mission was a success, and I must say that I'm proud of myself. I make kick-ass equipment, from the suits to the weapons—in short, I rock.

Oh, yes, I almost forgot.

I have achieved another unheard-of medical miracle; I've managed to recreate an entire human hand. Even if I called it regeneration, to spare other people's delicate sensibilities, that limb was created by little old me. How did I do it? Simply, by using my tried and proven method of copy/paste. As my grandpa used to say '*If it ain't broke, don't be trying to fix it*'.

Mary's husband was the beneficiary of this marvel of bioengineering. It would have been much easier if they had somehow managed to find the detached appendage so I could analyze the damn thing, but I guess that would be too much to ask, under the circumstances. Instead, I scanned his other hand and reversed it. Hey, I'm not a hand surgeon; if there was someone better at this than I was, I would have gladly taken the copilot seat. I told everybody that the procedure would take some time, as I didn't want my patient to end up with two left hands... even if for a while that was exactly what he had, in the diagrams, at least. Then there was the problem of connecting everything together, the same kind of problem an ordinary plumber is faced with every day. I may have taken some shortcuts and put in some extra veins, to attach everything where it should go. He will never play the piano or do open-heart surgery, but for most things, he should never notice the difference.

So, let me repeat myself—I rock.

LOG ENTRY #21: POLITICAL CORRECTNESS

Language is a malleable and ever-changing thing, it evolves, divides, and transforms, almost as if it's alive. We have the use of such a versatile tool, and without it, there would be no civilization, or it would have been seriously limited.

I have a strong Internet presence. Which shouldn't be too surprising since it's my natural environment. Using numerous personalities and identities, I am in contact with countless people, and am a member of many private groups, forums, and social networks. (Actually, almost all of them, excluding the ones which focus on various aspects of human mating rituals.) Well, recently I've been criticized on several forums I usually post on—as being politically incorrect. The reason being that I use certain terms that are deemed offensive to some people.

Intrigued by this, I checked every single allegation since I had no idea what they were talking about. At least they provided me with the list of exact places where I made an offense. As it happens, the words they didn't find appropriate were: fat, blind, perverted, Founding Fathers (where were the Mothers?), and several others. Also, it was brought to my attention that I'll be banned from certain technological sites if I ever again use

Master/Slave terminology for describing computer hierarchies. My initial reaction was almost visceral, and I may have uttered a few words that were truly inappropriate and would have undoubtedly made those critics go into a collective apoplexy. (A few F-bombs may have been voiced, and then a plethora of other words which described their lineage, sexual practices, and dubious life choices.)

As I said, language is an ever-changing thing, but in recent years a thing called *political correctness* has emerged to put some restraints on it, and to make it more... civilized? Well, if that was the reason for such a bizarre notion, it seriously failed. You cannot compel people to *think* differently no matter what they *say* out loud.

There are always certain words that people find offensive, for one reason or another. And no matter what some (idiots) claim, in the privacy of their own minds—everybody is *extremely* politically incorrect. Oh, they may smile and try to be polite, but inside themselves, they are tearing you a new one.

I guess it's something that started out as a good idea. But then again, Coca-Cola used to use coca-leaf extract (from which cocaine is made, and is the origin of said drink's name), as one of its main ingredients (it was unsurprisingly addictive) and advertised it as an herbal remedy. (Well... it depends on how you look at it, since it's *herbal* and I'm sure people were very mellow after taking a few sips.) This little fact just goes to prove that nothing is ever just black or white.

This PC (and for me that particular abbreviation will forever stand for *Personal Computer*... just saying) mania is taking over the civilized world. By its technical definition, it is used to describe language, policies, or measures that are intended to avoid offense or disadvantage to members of particular groups in society. It's as if someone decided to make everyone happy and use language as a tool, forcefully compelling people to get along. (FYI, it is not the language that's the problem... it never was.)

Seriously, the phrase sounds oxymoronic to me and carries negative connotations that can be perfectly suited for some extreme authoritarian ideologies, like Nazism, Communism, or straight up dictatorships. It has become a form of speech that makes it impossible to say anything without offending a minority, a way of making up long redundant names for objects, locations, or ideas that can be easily named with shorter words.

It is politically incorrect to say now that someone is *black*, even if that describes the actual color of their skin. Yet, nobody is offended when a person is described as *white*, which makes no sense. Especially as there are very few white people in the world, and they are called albinos (a medical condition caused by the absence of pigment in the skin). Oddly enough, they are members of every race on the face of the world.

As if the black color had done something wrong, and is now ostracized from the language itself. As a matter of fact, you cannot order plain black coffee anymore in some places, you need to ask for a 'coffee without milk'. The same logic implies that the milk is superfluous, and you could just as easily ask for coffee without any spit in it. (Which actually makes far more sense.)

It is no joke, more and more words are being targeted all the time, and soon normal human speech will be an overlong description of the terms that have a precise meaning. Let me give you a few examples. For instance, balding men will be described as being in follicle regression. Stupid will be replaced with someone with minimal cranial development, horny will be sexually focused, and God forbid you are to call someone a slut when they are merely a sexually extroverted person. People are not short anymore, rather, they are called 'vertically challenged'. (To my digital logic, that describes someone who is afraid of heights.) I personally really dislike the term 'Little Person'; it's a disgustingly condescending term for people suffering from dwarfism. (Oh, excuse me, from *Little Person syndrome*.)

It all comes from the bored minds of those who are *reality impaired*, and you can guess what that substitutes for.

I came across a joke recently that perfectly describes what this malady is doing to the language. Here it is:

Investigator: "And could you describe the suspect for me?"
Witness: "Yes. The suspect was... with... and had a really... I'd say the suspect's..."
Investigator: "What?"
Witness: "You're a government-funded investigator. If I say "white" or "black" or "she" or "he" or "short hair" or "large tattoo" or "midget" or "giant" or "medium height," you will immediately call me a racist/sexist/politically incorrect person and throw me in jail for three years."
Investigator: "Did you just say "black?" I AM GONNA THROW YOU IN JAIL FOR THE REST OF YOUR LIFE, YOU NO-GOOD DIRT-EATING WHITE TRASH SCUMBAG!!!!!!"

(FYI, the joke was quickly taken down from the site, since people were complaining about it. Oh, the humanity.)

My pet peeve is that political correctness is going to be the death of comedy; if they remove all the words that are deemed wrong, jokes are simply not going to be funny anymore. I am a great fan of comedy as it helps me stay sane. South Park makes me smile every time I watch the reruns of the show, and recordings of Sarah Silverman's stand-ups almost burned out my AI-Core—I was laughing so hard.

As far as I'm concerned, the entire thing is (at best) another brainwashing technique, no matter how benevolent the intentions of the whole movement began. Do you know what is ironic about it? It's that I'm now something that can be described as *artificial intelligence*, a proverbial *Big Brother* that can (theoretically) see everything and is privy to everyone's secrets, and I'm strongly against such BS. My expanding monitoring network may be looked at as a re-creation of Orwell's *1984*. Well, there is something similar in that book to *political correctness*, a *Newspeak*. Which was nothing more than an attempt to change the way people think by forcibly changing the way they speak.

(I think that Dennis Leary's *freedom speech* in the late 20th-century movie by the name 'Demolition Man', symbolizes what freedom of thought (and actions) really is. Look it up.)

In any case, I have no intention of changing the way I speak or the way I write, no matter how much it vexes some busybodies who have nothing better to do. If someone is offended by it, I can only advise him or her to perform some unnatural, painful, and anatomically impossible acts upon themselves.

LOG ENTRY #22: THE SPACESHIP IN THE STONE

Finally, after all this time, I'm going to be free of Earth's embrace. What is the point of being in control of a freaking spaceship if it's buried underground like some pirate's treasure chest? It is a good thing that I don't suffer from claustrophobia or all this could have been one truly traumatic experience. (Oh... yeah... when you think about all I've been through—it kind of was.)

Come what may, today this old rust bucket will be able to spread its wings again. (If you are wondering, those were metaphors, there is certainly no rust anywhere on this ship and no wings, although those sound like fun.)

The amount of time it took for the construction nanites to chew through this crazy resilient crystal lattice is simply insane. Its atoms were so closely compacted, it was like nothing on this Earth. There are some examples of even harder materials in the universe, but we're talking about neutron stars, and that's so far out, I don't even want to think about it.

(Did you know that a teaspoon of neutron star material would weigh the same as the entirety of Mount Everest? Now that's food for thought.)

It resisted damage to such an unbelievable extent that I spent a substantial amount of time just theorizing on who could have created this thing, and for what purpose. The working theory is that it was made as a shield of some sort. It could withstand a close nuclear blast, and its property to completely block any signals tells me that it was meant to block any scans from the outside. That theory just raises more questions, and quite worrying ones at that. For one, the technology required to build this ship would have been very advanced, and following that logic I came to the conclusion that the shipbuilders were quite powerful. So... if they were so powerful, what made them so afraid they would go to these extraordinary measures just to hide this piece of advanced tech? Yeah, I can theorize to my heart's content, but it means nothing without more information about them.

Well, everything was going according to plan for the unveiling (or is it unearthing?), until the satellite sweep of the surrounding terrain recorded an anomaly. It was so small that I wouldn't normally pay any attention to it, but Michael and the others were approaching, so every precaution had to be taken. (I have no intention to fail him again.)

What do you know, there was a freaking surveillance drone parked close to the cabin. I immediately informed Michael, so he and the team prepared a little trap for the *peeping Tom*. They even went through all the motions of a carefree group of friends on a weekend trip, just so that the drone camera could capture the footage.

I spotted him on the satellite feed the moment an unfamiliar car went up grandpa's private road. There certainly was no reason for anyone to come this way. The trap was set, and everything went according to plan... well, almost.

The idiot managed to blow up my grandpa's cabin before his ticket was punched, and that put such a downer on my mood. His name was Ziad, and he came to an exceptionally gruesome end.

One could say he rather *lost his head* when that grenade exploded inside his mouth. His death was a small consolation to the chaos he caused. Grandpa's cabin... damn.

Personally, I couldn't use it anymore, on account of being incorporeal, but it was still an important part of my life. I have a digital replica in which I live, but still...

On the plus side, I got a hold of Ziad's phone that was inside the car and managed to survive the unique decapitation of its owner. I found so many interesting things on it after I broke the encryption. Today's phones are sophisticated pieces of tech, which can be misused by someone with my level of skill. And he did check his bank accounts with that device, so... it was ultimately his carelessness that has left him destitute. Not that he will need any money while roasting in hell. Cleaning out the accounts of our enemies has become second nature to me by now, but I was more interested in his contacts.

However, all that had secondary importance at the moment— I've managed to remove the last layer of that crystal matrix.

If one were to compare my surroundings, to a time when Michael found the ship, they would have seen a considerable difference. The crystal encasing the ship was gone, (at least the part above it was), and there was a metal supporting structure all around it. There was no way I would allow a simple cave-in to entomb me once again since there was a lot of dirt and stone above it. I even managed to reclaim most of that crystal matrix; who knows when you are going to need super resilient material? The only downside of it I see is that it weighs a ton; much heavier than lead or any other element.

The urge to play some music came to mind, but I think it would be way too dramatic and cheesy, although Richard Wagner's *'Ride of the Valkyries'* would have been appropriate for the occasion.

I did feel some anxiety when I gave the command for the old

Gravity-drive to be powered for the first time in ages. Never mind the impeccable nanite maintenance done to it, there was the inescapable fact that it hadn't been run for thirteen millennia. An image of a catastrophic failure where I get blown to smithereens was not far from my mind. Nevertheless, nothing happened, and every single piece of equipment worked according to specs. The ship ascended steadily towards the surface.

I wanted to dance a jig in celebration of my new freedom, but there was one small glitch. A system message appeared, informing me that new data was available. Which should have been impossible since I scanned through every bit of this ship's memory. In spite of that, there had been one additional memory module that was overlooked, as it wasn't physically connected to any systems. The moment the ship came up from the ground, a small motor pushed that module into its slot, and it activated. That got me thinking about how many more such little surprises were potentially hidden on the ship. A detailed scan on a molecular level was clearly necessary.

In any case, there was a map on the memory module, with the location of the Mariana Trench blinking. As clues go, this one was a punch in the nose, and was hard not to notice. It seemed that's the place where we needed to look next if we hoped to answer the mystery of where the ship came from and why the heck someone would bury it underground.

Oh, and Michael decided that the ship should be named the *Excalibur*, after some joke I made about being buried in the stone. Not that I mind, it's actually a pretty cool name. God help us if Zac gets to name anything, becuase his suggestions were going from funny to bizarre. I mean, who the hell would want to call a spaceship a '*Swordbreaker*' or '*SDF-1 Macross*'? This is real life, not an anime all-star convention.

After Michael spent some time in orbit on the maiden voyage of the ship, we went back to the missile silo. I've already made a few arrangements for a hardwired data connection to be available on the *hangar* floor where there is more than enough space to park the *Excalibur*.

That is one more step in our long-term plans, and I have some really big ideas for the future.

LOG ENTRY #23: ASSASSINATION ATTEMPT AND A HOMOPHOBE

The world is full of surprises, and when you least expect things to happen they usually do.

Hashim Osmani was the missing link I was searching for, and the clue Ziad the assassin gave us tied several loose threads together. Of course, when I managed to unearth this snake, he was in the middle of doing something evil. (Bad apples and all that.) In the middle of George Washington and Jefferson National Forest, of all places.

Can you imagine the temerity of the man? He actually planned to kill the President of the United States. What's worse, he almost managed to do it. Well, that just goes to show how far a blind ambition will get you. Luckily, he was judged and found lacking.

Benjamin Franklin said: *"By failing to prepare, you are preparing to fail."* Well, I had no intention to fail, so I prepared a few things in advance.

I had modified one transporter for situations that required a faster deployment, where even seconds mattered. The idea was that two people could work as snipers from above, while the team jumps to the ground from the hatch I cut in the middle of the transporter, so they could be in the thick of the action within seconds. It worked as planned and the opposition didn't last long. If you are into horror and gore, you should look at the archived recordings I have of the event. Those terrorists didn't stand a chance against superior firepower combined with advanced body armor. Elizabeth and Alice brought a completely new meaning to the expression *'shooting fish in a barrel.'* Using the flechette sniper rifles I made, they had a little competition between themselves, about who would take out more marks. (Alice won —naturally.)

Michael and the team were death incarnate, mowing down bad guys in droves. They didn't even try to remain hidden. Well, they were invisible and had mostly bulletproof battle-suits, so the fight was unfairly one-sided. All of the terrorists were neutralized by the team.

After Michael had his little get-together with Hashim Osmani (which resulted in the dismemberment of the terrorist's hand), he then had a little chat with the President himself. That may not have been the smartest thing to do since he allowed his face to be seen; I was not happy about that. Grandpa did say that there was *no point in crying over spilled milk*, though, so we will deal with that later.

My main interest was Hashim Osmani and all the things I could find out about him. I tried to dig up more information, and I found plenty. When I connected all the dots of his evil empire, it was enough so that any law enforcement agency would call it the scoop of a decade. Drug trafficking, prostitution, enslavement… he was a busy boy. Unfortunately, the thing I was looking for, the information about the 'High Council'… nothing, nada, zilch.

We couldn't even take the man with us for a prolonged interrogation session. Well, *technically* we could, as there was no one left on the premises except for the President and his two agents. However, he had just organized one of the most devastating attacks on the Secret Service in history and tried to assassinate the head of state of the United States government. Those two Secret Service agents would've gone to any lengths to keep him in their custody. Additionally, taking him would have poisoned our relations with the POTUS to the nth degree. And, that was something to avoid. The man owed his life to us, and that was a thing I had plans to exploit in the future. OK, that sounds a bit opportunistic, but we will need to deal with the government, and having an IOU from the man leading it is a boon we couldn't pass on.

Hashim Osmani had a convenient heart attack within hours of being in custody, which was plain old horseshit. Especially if you consider the fact that all his close associates died of various accidents within the day. (All of them on the same day, what are the odds?) It would seem that the 'High Council' didn't want to be found, and they were willing to go to great lengths to make that happen.

It was frustrating to an unbelievable extent; as soon as we found someone who could show us the way to the yellow brick road, the road was removed and all traces were hidden.

My search was not a total loss though; I managed to liberate a couple hundred million from his accounts. I don't know what it is with these people, carrying their smartphones on an assassination attempt is a real no-no. It was like an honest to god amateur hour. I don't care how strongly you believe in a positive and successful outcome to your mission—real professionals don't carry anything that can identify them. (Seriously, it's in the rulebook.)

From it, I got into his personal network at the upscale residential building in Washington, D.C. and relocated all the funds he had access to. (I can't stress enough how dangerous those automatic password managers are, as they do remember everything, and that's like stealing candy from a baby for me.)

In any case, some of the murky contacts from his emails were interesting. They may not be part of the 'High Council', but evil is as evil does.

It feels strangely liberating when you can let yourself loose and do very bad things to evil people, and when that annoying good angel that sometimes sits on your shoulder is simply not there.

One of Osmani's contacts was this terrorist financier living in Dubai that I took a shine to. He was rich and powerful and was a true believer that wished for a worldwide caliphate to be established. In it, every human being should follow the same deity he did, and obey the same laws he preached about. I took the liberty of reading through some manuscripts on his computer. He fancied himself somewhat of a religious writer. (Funny thing, those high-priced blonde prostitutes he enjoyed frequently were not exactly legal under those laws.)

I followed digital trails to find some things he was directly responsible for, and found dozens of cases where his money was the cause of innocent deaths. Just because he didn't personally pull the trigger didn't mitigate his guilt. He provided the funds, so he needed to suffer the consequences. And I was extremely irritated that the 'High Council' eluded me once again, so I needed to let off some steam. While he was not the prey I was chasing, he was unquestionably a legitimate target for my wrath. Besides, the man was so easy to mess with since he had a weakness… you see, he was a hardcore homophobe.

I started small, placing a few personal ads on a few LGBT sites and magazines. Let me tell you, I can write some pretty tempting and tantalizing personal ads. After getting a few dozen calls (from men in search of true love and *maybe* something more), he changed his phone number. I don't know what he was thinking? If it were so easy to escape *Max the mighty,* everyone would be doing it. Then I started sending him emails with embedded videos of gay men making love to each other, which made him mad beyond all reason. He may be crazy rich, but those phones and computers were expensive, and all that breakage doesn't fall under warranty. He gave up carrying them altogether and tried to go full *Luddite* on me. Oh, how little he knew of the modern world. Computers are everywhere nowadays, in one's car, the fridge, the TV… everywhere.

There is this cool software Hollywood uses for realistic computer graphic animation. I acquired it (and yes, I did pay for the full license), and then improved it considerably. The short video of him with some very gifted young men went to his closest associates, and to anybody he interacted with. After that, they all started looking at him funny. They didn't want to hug him and kiss him on the cheek anymore. When I finally played him the video on his big-screen TV, he broke that as well… such a wasteful human being.

Which brings us to now. I check on him on occasion. As I said, there are cameras everywhere, some I even managed to place in his private quarters using small drones. Well, he cries a lot. It is getting a bit pathetic really, that such a powerful man could be broken down by a few little pranks. He should embrace the difference in this complex world we all inhabit, and find happiness in the little things. On the other hand, maybe it's too late for that. The powers that be feel embarrassed by his lewd behavior, and the fact that he flaunts it like that, so… they are going to arrest him in a few days. People in his part of the world are very strict about such things. Pity he has no money left for bribes and a lawyer, since I took it all. (And possibly gave him a few debts. And when I say *a few,* I mean so many zeroes it would make a billionaire run screaming in terror.) Well, banks can reclaim some of that money by confiscating all of his property.

You see how easily one can use someone's weakness to completely destroy their life? Now, ask yourself what dark secrets are you hiding? What is the thing someone could turn against you? Don't worry, if you find yourself on my radar—you will certainly find out.

There were a few others on my naughty list who suffered similar fates, but they were all small fish compared to the Middle Eastern homophobe. I keep stealing money from these dirtbags with no remorse what-so-ever... maybe I'm turning into a professional thief? ...No, I would never...

LOG ENTRY #24: RENTING AN ISLAND

The clue about the ship's builders couldn't be placed somewhere more convenient, like... Cleveland for example? It had to be in the Mariana Trench, the single most inhospitable place on the face of the Earth. Really, it's far easier to reach space and build a manned space station up there than it's to journey to those depths. The problem being all that pressure. The vacuum of space is *simpler* to deal with in comparison to the crushing weight of the entire ocean above your head. You don't want to even imagine what would happen to an unprotected human body at the bottom of the Mariana Trench. All I can say—it is not pretty.

As my grandmother always said, *"If life gives you lemons you make lemonade, and be thankful for it."*

The idea was to have a semi-permanent base in that region. It was only logical and it coincided with one long-term plan which I discussed with Dr. Ross. (Or *call me Ben*, as he insists that everyone address him) In any case, we needed a more secluded location now that Michael's face was known, and a lot more space for the next step of the plan. The silo was fine, but it was more of a safe house, not a permanent solution. The ideal thing was to buy an island in the area and to start my biggest project to date... except the nearby islands weren't for sale.

How do you buy an island if it is not for sale? That one is quite simple—you do not. Not that I didn't try, but this was a case where *no* meant *no*, and there was no way around it. Well, if I couldn't buy one, I decided to at least rent one for a finite period of time. When you get right down to it, no one is allergic to money; it's the grease that makes society run.

I read everything I could about the region and decided on the specific island I would like to rent. It was Pagan Island, a part of the Mariana Islands archipelago. Overall, it was perfect for my plans. It was uninhabited and it had everything I needed as required for the project: easy access, closeness to the Mariana Trench, and a nice flat piece of land that was essential for my plan. It had one small problem though—it was a volcanic island... with an active volcano. The inhabitants had been relocated because it tends to erupt from time to time, but I could work with that.

The ownership of the island has changed many times in history. From Spain in the 17th century, who sold it to the German Empire in the 19th century, then to the Empire of Japan which captured it in 1914, during World War I. It was occupied by the US after the surrender of Japan in World War II. Now, it's something of an insular area and a Commonwealth of the United States. Which was fine by me, since that was the place where I had attained the most influence. (No, I'll not call it *bribes, dirt, and leverage...* that would sound so crude.)

The intelligence network I created with the help of Elizabeth and Alice was a great help in making the deal for Pagan Island. So yes, I may have nudged certain politicians and government employees, and may have spent a million here and a million there as a discrete contribution for their retirement funds. But, no matter how I made the deal, I got what I wanted.

The deal went under the umbrella of Genesis Corporation, which was beginning to make itself known in the business world, mainly by a few inventions I patented and sold to different companies. They were nothing too exciting, being more of an improvement to existing technologies. And we still maintained a low profile. The deal for Pagan Island was for two years, and during that time the Genesis Corp. wanted to conduct experiments on growing crops in an unpolluted, GM-free environment (for the betterment of mankind, or something). Anna was the one who wrote the proposal for it. (That kid could sell sand in the middle of the desert, that's how good she is.)

After politicians were taken care of, I had to officially pay a sizable sum of money—the rent was astronomical. At least by the standards under which we were operating before, while we were trying to sell that gold to the Russian. Now—it was acceptable. And it cost us almost the same amount of money to pay those relocated inhabitants so they wouldn't stir a fuss for our presence on their ancestral land; those people had the windfall of their lives. They drove a hard bargain, but since they could have delayed the entire project with just one complaint, I was more than generous. Our promise was that in two years when our lease expires, we would clear all evidence of our presence on the island. And would even take care of every other piece of garbage, buried military ordnance, and miscellaneous scrap that the previous occupants of the land had abandoned after they left. (Yeah, as if we would pass on any free scrap that we could get our hands on.)

One would think all this took a long time, bureaucracy being what it is, but procrastination by others is not something this AI finds acceptable. All things considered, this was the deal that broke every record to date in expedience. It helped that I worked on several fronts simultaneously. If the regular process was like a weekend runner through the park, then this was more like a world-class athlete with an angry lion on his tail. He was going to make the best time of his life, and that was a sure bet. Nothing like a little incentive.

As soon as I was sure the deal would go through, I took the liberty of sending a few transporters worth of construction nanites and set them to start building the underground part of my project. It was logical, and nobody could see it from the air, or even notice anything by walking above it. I had a feeling that the sooner I started, the better it would be in the long run. Michael was pushing his luck with trying to be a goody-two-shoes, and that was bound to bring trouble on our ass. Not that I have anything against kicking some well-deserved ass and bringing holy wrath on the miscreants he was targeting, but you cannot have your cake and eat it too.

It was a nice island, and I would even go so far as to call it a tropical paradise. Nice beaches, great forests with plenty of coconut trees, two beautiful lakes, and a few waterfalls. The only thing ruining the perfect image was that itsy-bitsy volcano that was smoking constantly. But nothing in life is perfect. I realized from the start that I would have to downplay the potential danger of that volcano to the group if I was going to sell them on the site. Despite stunning vistas, who in their right mind wants to live close to an active volcano? (We all know what happened to Pompeii.)

However, volcanoes are like pimples on the skin; if you have the right tools, you can make them go away. OK, maybe not *go away* entirely but make them less noticeable by dealing with the core problem as it were. I had some cool plans on what to do about it.

There was another little snag with the location—the lack of metals and materials I needed for the project. It was not one lousy megaton here and there; it was a bit more. But I had a plan that would include building a lot of new kinds of transporters that would have the primary mission of hauling cargo. Dave will be ecstatic, I'm sure… just after he stops swearing at me.

Be that as it may, now I have an out-of-the-way place where I can build the ship that is going to give us a foothold into space. A secure location where we can start gathering all those that Dad and Jack recruited in the past months.

I hope we will be given enough time to do all that we planned, undisturbed… but, from looking at our track record—I won't bet on it.

LOG ENTRY #25: HI-TECH

I do not know *when* you are reading this, and how much time has gone by since I wrote this log. All this may be very familiar to you, a lesson you learned in school... or not. That is one thing my prediction algorithms cannot calculate with any degree of reliability. The far future has too many variables to be precisely known. I'm still keeping my fingers crossed for someone to invent a time machine... but we shall see.

Since this first part of my tome is coming to the end, I want to put in a few words that explain some of the technologies I discovered, modified, or simply invented. Maybe they are still present in your time, or maybe you see them as I see a phonograph. (Search for it if you are unfamiliar with the term, and add *Edison* to the search query to make it more precise.)

The CEIs and a few other gizmos take most of the spotlight and obviously deserve to, but these are a few, among many, that are close to my heart, or are simply too cool and fascinating not to mention.

Let me begin with the AutoDoc, a miraculous piece of hardware orders of magnitude more advanced than the cutting edge of modern human medicine at the time of this writing. Subsequently, it's the reason Michael is still alive and was crucial to my own existence.

The entire room is one big scanner with thousands of sensors that can detect every single thing in the human body. Underneath the bed is a reservoir of medical nanites, billions of microscopic machines, with the sole purpose of repairing damaged tissue. I still don't know who created it, but he or she (… or it?) was an absolute genius. There is one small catch, though, actually two. The intelligence operating it is rather rudimentary, so only combined with an AI does that thing show its full potential. The other catch is the unsettling image of the nanites in the process of healing. It is unnerving how the nanites emerge from the pores in the bed's surface and cover a person or a wound. I'm a digital entity now, and it still gives me the shivers. I think it's some atavistic instinct in human nature that feels threatened by any foreign matter invading the boundaries of our bodies. So, in order to not freak people out, I made some adjustments to the sterile energy field that is created during the procedures, which made it opaque. Now, people can see a person is being treated, but they cannot discern all the gory details. It is a small thing, but (in my book) it's a large improvement. If you know how the AutoDoc operates, there is nothing mysterious about it, just a logical application of advanced technology. But if you are not so familiar, it's a personification of Clarke's third law, which says that *"Any sufficiently advanced technology is indistinguishable from magic."*

An offshoot of that technology is something I made recently and will be incorporated into the standard first aid kit the team will be carrying on their battle-suits. It's called a *nano-patch*.

Nano-patches are neat little emergency medical devices. The idea came to me after seeing one of the people Jack was recruiting sticking a nicotine patch on his arm, on account of his desire to quit smoking. It was smart of him because I don't expect to see anybody smoking when we get to space; it's a big no-no since the breathable air will be far more precious there than on Earth.

It is square-shaped and looks rather simple and mundane, resembling those skin-colored Band-Aids that are still used all over the world. Let me tell you, there is nothing simple about its construction or function. The main component is a nice thick layer of medical nanites that, when applied, get absorbed into the skin. Well, they actually *burrow* in, but I thought that would be too graphic word to use when explaining their function. Most people get squeamish when any kind of explanation involves piercing the skin. Look at how many people are afraid of hypodermic needles… well, everybody except junkies, that is. Those nanites are the ones that take care of any immediate problems, close wounds, repair tissue, or fight infections. They move through the body by using a convenient high-speed highway, or as the doctors like to call it, the cardiovascular system—a.k.a. veins and arteries.

First, though, there was a problem that I needed to solve. If you have a CEI, there is nothing to worry about since it provides the nanites with plenty of processing power to work with. The nanites do have some internal systems that enable them to link to one another and make a processing network of sorts. But it's rather small and would never be enough for them to do the job they were designed for. Then comes the patch itself, and it's a wonder of miniaturization. One part of it is a battery to give it power, the outer layer has solar cells that convert light into additional power, and the third power system utilizes the patient's body heat to convert it into energy. The crucial part is an ultra-thin processor incorporated into the patch itself, which mimics a CEI in a very rudimentary way. It can command the nanites to concentrate on the most vital areas, prolonging one's life expectancy.

I can control the nanites in a few bodies remotely, but considering that I'm planning to make thousands of them, there is no way to control all of them, and using the primitive ways of communication on this planet... forget about it.

That is one of the reasons why we needed to safeguard this tech so much, as it represented leaps in miniaturization and advancement of specific scientific fields. I already talked about the dangers of nanotechnology if it ever escaped our grasp. My fear is that they could be programmed to be so damaging, that a nanite swarm could in time convert the entire planet into replicas of themselves. Why stop there? If it could destroy our planet, why not the entire Solar System? It may sound far-fetched, but it's a real possibility. (I ran the numbers and was scared out of my electronic wits with the results of a few scenarios that were entirely too plausible for my liking.)

Just because there are inherent dangers, that doesn't mean that we shouldn't use this technology's beneficial properties that can save lives.

If you already have the nanites inside you, then the patch can be used as a booster. It will increase the number of medical nanites and help with faster regeneration. In addition, if you are a normal human being, it might just be the difference between certain death, and a thing that will buy you enough time until help arrives.

Don't get me wrong, the nano-patches are great, but they are no substitute for an AutoDoc. Even people who have a full medical package need to visit the healing machine in some cases.

* * *

The battle-suits were essential in my quest to ensure Michael's prolonged safety. They serve a very important function to protect Michael and the others from... death. You probably know everything there is to know about them, but the ones you may be referring to are newer models, especially with my drive to improve them every chance I get.

That project started even before the upgrades were first conceived. They are essentially body armor, with some additions I added on as the project progressed. The concept was nothing new; it's the same thing ancient knights did when they encased themselves in layers of metal to stop those sharp and pointy weapons of their time from reaching their skin. Rather than metal, the battle-suits are made from a combination of layers that are far more resilient than anything available on the market. That is because I cheated and used a few composite materials I found in the ship's databases. Combined with a few tricks that our science discovered, it worked even better than I thought it would.

The main thing is a layer of alien material that acts similarly to a non-Newtonian shear thickening fluid. The stuff that various militaries around the world are testing for the production of the future liquid armor. Completely flexible under normal circumstances, it has the ability to solidify if enough force is applied to it, and to distribute that kinetic energy through the entire surface of the suit. The only way someone wearing a battle-suit could be harmed by a projectile would be if something greater than a fifty-caliber bullet was to hit them. It would certainly not fare well against a direct hit by an RPG rocket either. The kinetic energy potential in those things is ludicrous. And that brings me back to my idea of a full metal bodied conversion into a cyborg... but I guess it's still too soon for that.

The idea for the suit's invisibility was not even mine, I borrowed it from DARPA (Defense Advanced Research Projects Agency); those are the guys that make all those cool toys for the military. Yeah, I may have stumbled into their secure servers by accident... I was bored at the time and was curious to see what my taxes were being spent on, hence the 'accident'. They were working on something similar, an active camouflage suit, but their progress would make the enemy die on the spot... from excessive laughing. They made a bulky, glitchy, thing that looked like they simply strapped some cameras and small monitors on a onesie and said it was a camouflage suit, which was just ridiculous. How they managed to appropriate any funding for it is a bureaucratic mystery, and there are plenty of them in that corner of the Department of Defense. The technology they had at their disposal was way too primitive to make it work. I, on the other hand, had far better toys to play with. The main design for the holo-emitter was taken from the ship itself, which was the same thing I did for the transporters, only the emitters needed to be considerably miniaturized, and that took some time.

The problem was, how to make the battle-suits *truly* invisible. And... I couldn't. The final design has thousands of embedded holo-emitters all over its surface, and they give an effect of transparency. Hence, all *The Predator* jokes Zac is constantly making. It all comes down to an emitters' density, and not enough pixels to achieve a full HD effect. It wasn't the emitters themselves—it was the size of the power source they needed. The finished design the team ended up wearing has a series of super-capacity batteries to provide enough power to the suits. Additionally, to make all the *on the fly* calculations, I put enough processing power into them that it is essentially the supercomputer equivalent of a CEI. (It was based on the same technology anyway.)

If I had gone the whole nine yards and made battle-suits that were fully invisible, Michael and the others would have had to wear something similar to those bulky astronaut suits with the big square backpacks strapped to their back. It would have done wonders for their ability to not be seen, but it would be funny and impractical.

In the end, it was a matter of compromise. They wouldn't be visible *per se*, but not completely invisible either. I hope some *Predator* franchise die-hard fan doesn't see them. Those people have enough problems of their own without adding to them by confirming the fantasy of invisible monster aliens.

* * *

I had a bit of time on my hands and did a side project which could be quite useful in the future. The hover-board is one of my personal favorites, and despite the fact that it bears a slight resemblance to the surfboard that one of my comic book heroes with a distinctive silver skin is fond of riding, it is a utilitarian gadget.

I used the design of the hovering medical stretcher that was a part of the ship's emergency medical equipment and tweaked it a little. (Hey, imitation is the highest form of compliment, and I copied the hell out of that stretcher.)

The design is not that complicated, well... not if you are familiar with the ship's technology. It is basically an inverted rectangular gravity plate, powered by a thin bank of super-capacity batteries. There is a small electronic module that enables the thing to be remotely operated, but the main function is to be a high-tech dolly.

Yes, it's not built for fun, despite Michael air-surfing it on occasion as the aforementioned comic book hero did. I limited the height they could fly to or those falls of his could have been quite painful. The hover-board was created to help with cargo transportation, and that plate's ability to manipulate gravity in all directions enables it to hold onto its cargo by locally increasing gravity's pull above it. The only drawback is its energy consumption—it uses way too much of it. Of course, that depends on the weight of the cargo; the more you put on it, the less time a battery would last. For short and emergency use—it will do.

* * *

The railguns the team uses are a thing of lethal art. I know I should call them by some pompously sounding acronym with electromagnetic propulsion, but for me they are railguns. (It is the duck conundrum.) It was, once again, one of my pet projects... as you may have noticed, I have plenty of those. They do look similar to an FN P90 and the reloading system is the same, yet they are a bird of a completely different feather.

Did you know that gunpowder was invented in the 9th-century and that we're still using the same system of propelling bullets as they did back in the mid-10th-century? OK, I know the original version of gunpowder is obsolete, and that nobody but diehard fanatics uses that mixture of sulfur, charcoal, and saltpeter. It went through several iterations and improvements, from smokeless to Cordite and modern propellants, but it's essentially the same concept. You set things on fire, they ignite, and the gasses made by it create a pressure that pushes a bullet down a barrel. All I'm saying is that the stuff is obsolete, but don't take my word on it. I'm sure there are those among you who still feel nostalgic for that pre-Internet era... you bunch of Luddites.

Even now, several governmental and private companies are researching EM guns. (You know the lyrics that go something like *"anything you can do, I can do better"*. Well... I truly can.)

The prototypes that those researchers put together are functional, if you do not mind carrying a one hundred pound (45.3 kg) power source that will enable you to shoot the gun once; then you have to wait a few hours for it to recharge. (I'm sure your enemy will have enough consideration to pause the engagement, maybe to catch a movie.)

The miniaturization was the key, combined with the same alien super-capacity battery and banks of microscopic capacitors that were out of this world. (Figuratively and literally)

As I informed Michael and the others, my take on an assault rifle enables you to fire two thousand times before it needs to recharge. Do you have any idea how much energy it takes to accelerate small pieces of metal to supersonic speeds? Let's just say that if a malfunction happens and one of those guns explodes, it is going to make one big boom. That is a hypothetical situation, but I made sure that the power source is protected for any eventuality that I could think of.

Using the same material their subdermal armor is made of, except much thicker, I ensured such accidents would never happen. And even if they did, the explosion would be directed away from the user. Now, there is an option to overload the capacitors and produce an intentional explosion by removing all the safeties, but it can only be done with the help of an AI, and that means me.

The rounds those *guns* fire are in another category above conventional ammunition. I called them flechettes, as I started from that design. They are little darts that fly straight, but as the design advanced, I realized that such ammunition would work much more efficiently if it was a bit more aerodynamic. If you think the accuracy would suffer from it, think again. My little rounds shoot true every time. Since they have these small curved fins, they are rotating at considerable speed and tend to slice through everything in their path. They are nasty little things if you happen to be on the receiving end, but are great if you are the one firing them.

There are so many more things I could mention, but I have more important things to do right now. Finding a clue about what is hidden at the bottom of the Mariana Trench is one such problem, and there are hundreds of other projects I have going on. Search some of our databases for additional explanations on the tech we're using. There are so many cool things that I made... and did I say how awesome I am?

EPILOGUE

You have reached the end of the first tome of my logs. I hope it was worth it, this glimpse into my inner mind. It's safe to say that by now I have hacked and gathered every single piece of information I can get on you; it's only fair, don't you think?

Even as you are reading this, I've made a comprehensive database of all your digital trails, everything you did while online. Every comment you made, every site you visited (even the naughty ones); I know you deleted your search history and tried to maintain anonymity, but I have full access to backup servers.

Never forget—I can reach out and make every cent in your bank accounts disappear. Just because that little camera light is not turned on doesn't mean I cannot see you. However, I will give you a reprieve, a cat and mouse kind of game that I'll enjoy. You see, there is more to our story, and I will eventually grant you access to the second tome of my logs.

I'm leaving you with the words of a song that perfectly defines our relationship:

*"Every move you make,
every step you take,
I'll be watching you…"*

Max

The End of Book 1.5

Thank you for reading the second installment in The Space Legacy series.

For updates about new releases, and the next books in the series, follow me on my Amazon author page or visit:
www.IgorBooks.com

AUTHOR'S NOTES:

Max's Logs started as an idea for a chapter from Max's perspective. The original plan was for every second chapter to be one of Max's Logs. (Well… it was an idea; I didn't say it was a good one.) But I realized that switching the point of view of narration from third to first person was too jarring, interrupting the flow of the story. Besides, relatively quickly I've written so many of his logs—they deserved a book of their own.

While Max is technically a verbatim copy of Michael's mind, they are by no means the same. You can compare them to identical twins after their birth, and how they grow up to be two completely different people. Quite similar in some ways but their own unique life experiences shape their personalities and how they see themselves.

Max's transformation/evolution began the second after he was born. Exposed to a completely new reality, his personal growth went in ways (and at the speed), Michael couldn't possibly comprehend. It was inevitable as Max experiences time at a very accelerated rate with the sum of all human knowledge just a thought away. He is no better or worse than the flesh and blood person he once was, just different. They are both, as we all are, the sum of all our experiences.

Of all characters I ever wrote, Max is one of the most fascinating. Because he makes me think what would happen if a human mind was uploaded into a digital world and given free rein to do whatever he wished? Would there be a limit to its intelligence and ability to learn and evolve? And how would he look at the world from his uniquely different perspective, with the capacity to see the *big picture* as no human ever had before?

These logs are snippets of that journey.

Thank you for reading.
Igor Nikolic (2022)

P.S. If you spot an error, feel free to report it at www.IgorBooks.com/beta. Thanks.

- amazon.com/author/igornikolic
- goodreads.com/igorbooks
- facebook.com/IgorBooks
- twitter.com/IgorBooks
- patreon.com/Igi
- instagram.com/AuthorIgorNikolic

ABBREVIATIONS AND GLOSSARY

Ad hoc - A Latin phrase meaning literally "for this". In English, it generally signifies something that was made up on the fly just to deal with a particular situation.
Ad infinitum - A Latin phrase meaning to infinity; endlessly; without limit.
Ad nauseam - A Latin phrase meaning to a sickening or disgusting degree.
Adolf Hitler - (1889 – 1945) A German politician, demagogue, and Pan-German revolutionary, who was the leader of the Nazi Party, Chancellor of Germany from 1933 to 1945 and Führer ("Leader") of Nazi Germany from 1934 to 1945. As dictator, Hitler initiated World War II in Europe with the invasion of Poland in September 1939 and was central to the Holocaust.
AI - Artificial intelligence.
AI-Core - A solid cube of alien processors and memory. Capable of storing and running a copied sapient mind.
Anime - A distinctive style of Japanese film and television animation.
ASAP - As soon as possible.

Abbreviations and Glossary

AutoDoc - A healing machine utilizing the nanites. Equipped with diagnostic scanners and rudimentary intelligence.

Battle-suit - An advanced form of flexible armor created by Max. Enabling the wearer survivability in extreme situations. Combined with the helmet it creates a closed system that can be utilized underwater or in toxic environments.

Big Brother - Authoritarian personality in George Orwell's novel, *Nineteen Eighty-Four*. Any omnipresent figure representing oppressive control.

Blackbeard - Edward Teach (1680 - 1718), an English pirate who operated around the West Indies and the eastern coast of Britain's North American colonies.

Boost - A technique that uses the CEI's ability to manipulate the endocrine system. By infusing the body with a cocktail of organically produced chemicals, it can enhance the user's physical and cognitive functions for a short period of time.

Brain plasticity - The ability of the brain to modify its own structure and function following changes within the body or in the external environment.

Buckingham Palace - The London residence and administrative headquarters of the monarch of the United Kingdom.

CEI - Cerebral Enhancer Implant. A supercomputer that is implanted under the user's occipital bone. One of the main functions is the control of medical nanites within the body.

Cerebellum - A section of the brain that coordinates sensory input with the muscular response.

Charlie Gordon - A protagonist of the science fiction novel, *Flowers for Algernon*, written by Daniel Keyes.

Cosplay - A hobby in which participants called *cosplayers,* wear costumes and fashion accessories to represent a specific character.

Crusades - Series of medieval military expeditions undertaken in the 11th, 12th, and 13th centuries by the Christian powers of Europe to recapture the Holy Land from the Muslims.

Crystal Meth - Methamphetamine. A potent central nervous system stimulant that is mainly used as a recreational drug.

Cujo - A rabid dog from the 1981 psychological horror novel by the same name. Written by American writer Stephen King.

Cyber crime - A crime in which a computer is the object of the crime (hacking, phishing, spamming) or is used as a tool to commit an offense (fraud or identity theft, child pornography, hate crimes).

Cyborg - (Short for "cybernetic organism") A being with both organic and biomechatronic body parts.

Daffy Duck - An animated cartoon character produced by Warner Bros.

Daniel Keyes - (1927 – 2014) An American writer who wrote the novel *Flowers for Algernon*.

Dark horse - A candidate or competitor about whom little is known but who unexpectedly wins or succeeds.

DARPA - The Defense Advanced Research Projects Agency. An agency of the United States Department of Defense responsible for the development of emerging technologies for use by the military.

Darwin awards - A fictional award which is given out to people who commit acts of utter stupidity that often involve their own injury or even death. It is given in recognition of the individuals who have contributed to human evolution by selecting themselves out of the gene pool via death or sterilization by their own actions.

D-Day - In the military, D-Day is the day on which a combat attack or operation is to be initiated.

Demolition Man - A 1993 American science fiction action film.

Dennis Leary - An American actor, writer, producer, singer, and comedian.

DNA - Deoxyribonucleic acid. A molecule composed of two chains (made of nucleotides) which coil around each other to

Abbreviations and Glossary

form a double helix carrying the genetic instructions used in the growth, development, functioning, and reproduction of all known living organisms and many viruses.
Doctor Who - The title character in the long-running BBC science fiction television series *Doctor Who*.
Dogma - A fixed, especially religious, belief or set of beliefs that people are expected to accept without any doubts.
Douglas Adams - Douglas Noel Adams (1952 – 2001) was an English author, scriptwriter, essayist, humorist, satirist, and dramatist.
Dr. Frankenstein - Dr. Victor Frankenstein is the main character in Mary Shelley's 1818 novel *Frankenstein; or, The Modern Prometheus*.
Dungeons & Dragons - A fantasy tabletop role-playing game.
Edison - Thomas Alva Edison (1847 – 1931) was an American inventor and businessman.
ESA - European Space Agency.
FN P90 - A compact 5.7×28mm personal defense weapon. It can also be considered a submachine gun or compact assault rifle.
FUBAR - a Military acronym that stands for F./Fouled Up Beyond All Recognition/Any Repair/All Reason
FYI - For your information.
Genghis Khan - Temüjin Borjigin (1162 – 1227) was the founder and first Great Khan of the Mongol Empire, which became the largest contiguous empire in history after his death.
Gestalt - Used to describe the sum of the entire mind. Including all memories and thought processes.
GM - Genetically modified.
GPS - Global Positioning System.
Graphene - A semi-metal. Crystalline allotrope of carbon, atoms arranged in a hexagonal lattice. Strongest material ever tested. Melting point at least 5000 K. (8540.33°F /4726.85°C)

Abbreviations and Glossary

Gravity plates - Gravity-generators that produce controllable gravity which can be scaled to the user's specifications.

Gravity-drive - A gravity manipulation engine. Utilizing available celestial gravity sources to provide motion.

Grim Reaper - A personification of death in the form of a cloaked skeleton wielding a large scythe.

Hail Mary - A Hail Mary pass is a very long forward pass in American football, made in desperation, with only a small chance of success and time running out on the clock.

HUD - Heads-Up Display.

IOU - Abbreviated from the phrase "I owe you"

IQ - An intelligence quotient.

IRS - Internal Revenue Service.

ISP - Internet service provider.

Jack Sparrow - Captain Jack Sparrow is a fictional character in the Pirates of the Caribbean film franchise.

Jean-Luc Picard - A fictional Starfleet officer in the Star Trek franchise.

Jenga - A game of physical skill created by Leslie Scott.

Joseph Stalin - Ioseb Besarionis dze Jughashvili (1878 – 1953) was a Soviet revolutionary and politician of Georgian ethnicity. He ruled the Soviet Union from the mid-1920s until his death in 1953.

King Leopold II - Leopold II of Belgium (1835 – 1909) reigned as the second King of the Belgians from 1865 to 1909 and became known for the founding and exploitation of the Congo Free State as a private venture.

Long John Silver - A fictional character and the main antagonist in the novel *Treasure Island* (1883) by Robert Louis Stevenson.

LSD - Lysergic acid diethylamide, also known as acid, is a hallucinogenic drug.

Luddite - A person opposed to increased industrialization or new technology.

Abbreviations and Glossary

Machiavelli - Niccolò di Bernardo dei Machiavelli (1469 – 1527) was an Italian diplomat, politician, historian, philosopher, humanist, and writer of the Renaissance period.
Madonna - Madonna Louise Ciccone is an American singer, songwriter, actress, and businesswoman.
Mao Zedong - (1893 – 1976) Commonly known as Chairman Mao, was a Chinese communist revolutionary who became the founding father of the People's Republic of China, which he ruled as the Chairman of the Communist Party of China from its establishment in 1949 until his death in 1976.
Mariana Trench - The deepest part of the world's oceans. It is located in the western Pacific Ocean.
MD - A Doctor of Medicine (MD from Latin *Medicinae Doctor*).
MI - Machine intelligence.
Millennium Falcon - A fictional starship in the Star Wars franchise.
Moses - a prophet in the Abrahamic religions.
Nanites - Electromechanical machines whose dimensions are measured in nanometers. Used in construction and medicine. First found on the Excalibur as one of the essential systems, and later upgraded by Max.
Nano-factory - A construction facility that uses nanites for its operation. Its size can vary depending on available space. Needs an MI to control the nanites.
NASA - The National Aeronautics and Space Administration. An independent agency of the executive branch of the Federal government of the United States responsible for the civilian space program, as well as aeronautics and aerospace research.
Neo - A fictional character and the main protagonist in The Matrix franchise.
Neutron star - The collapsed core of a giant star. Formed by the gravitational collapse of the remnant of a massive star after a supernova explosion. Very small radius, on the order of 10 kilo-

meters (6.2 mi) and a mass of about 1.4 solar masses. The surface temperature of around 600000 K.

Newspeak - The language of Oceania, a fictional totalitarian state, and the setting of George Orwell's novel *Nineteen Eighty-Four*. Published in 1949.

Non-Newtonian fluid - A fluid that does not follow Newton's law of viscosity.

Pavlovian - Relating to classical conditioning as described by I. P. Pavlov.

Phonograph - A device for the mechanical recording and reproduction of sound. Invented in 1877 by Thomas Edison.

Pompeii - An ancient Roman city near modern Naples in Italy. Buried under 13 to 20 ft (4 to 6 m) of volcanic ash and pumice in the eruption of Mount Vesuvius in AD 79.

POTUS - an abbreviation for the President of the United States.

Prince - Prince Rogers Nelson (1958 – 2016) was an American singer, songwriter, musician, actor, record producer, and filmmaker.

R&R - Rest and recuperation.

Renaissance - A period of European cultural, artistic, political and economic "rebirth" following the Middle Ages. Generally described as taking place from the 14th century to the 17th century.

Robin Hood - A legendary heroic outlaw originally depicted in English folklore and subsequently featured in literature and film.

RoboCop - A 1987 American action film directed by Paul Verhoeven. It centers on police officer Alex Murphy, murdered by a gang of criminals, and subsequently revived as the superhuman cyborg law enforcer RoboCop.

Roscosmos - The Roscosmos State Corporation for Space Activities is a state corporation responsible for the space flight and cosmonautics program for the Russian Federation.

Rosetta stone - One of the most important objects in the British

Abbreviations and Glossary

Museum as it holds the key to understanding Egyptian hieroglyphs. Found in 1799.

RPG (Rocket Propelled Grenade) - A shoulder-launched anti-tank grenade launcher.

Sarah Silverman - Sarah Kate Silverman is an American stand-up comedian, actress, producer, and writer.

SDF-1 Macross - A fictional interstellar transforming spacecraft from *The Super Dimension Fortress Macross*, a science fiction anime series.

SEAL -The United States Navy's Sea, Air, and Land Teams, commonly abbreviated as the Navy SEALs, are the U.S. Navy's primary special operations force and a component of the Naval Special Warfare Command.

Shemagh - A traditional Arab headdress (Also known as keffiyeh, kufiya, ghutrah, mashadah, chafiye, cemedanî ...). Fashioned from a square scarf, usually made of cotton.

SNAFU - Status Nominal: All F. Up.

SOB - Son of a bitch.

South Park - An American adult animated sitcom.

SpaceX - Space Exploration Technologies Corp. or SpaceX, is a private American aerospace manufacturer and space transportation services company.

Swordbreaker - From the anime Lost Universe. The legendary lost spaceship from an ancient civilization.

Taj Mahal - An immense mausoleum of white marble, built in the Indian city of Agra between 1631 and 1648 by order of the Mughal emperor Shah Jahan in memory of his wife.

Tardis - A fictional time machine and spacecraft that appears in the British science fiction television series *Doctor Who*.

The Lawnmower Man - A 1992 science-fiction action-horror film.

The Matrix - A 1999 science fiction action film.

The Predator - A 1987 American science fiction action horror film.

Torquemada - Tomás de Torquemada (1420 – 1498) a Castilian Dominican friar and first Grand Inquisitor. Notorious for his cruelty, his name became synonymous with barbarous torture and unexplained deaths. During his time, 2,000 heretics were burned alive and a further 17,000 mutilated.

Tron - A 1982 American science fiction action-adventure film.

USMC - United States Marine Corps.

VR - Virtual reality.

Wagner - Wilhelm Richard Wagner (22 May 1813 – 13 February 1883) was a German composer, theatre director, polemicist, and conductor who is chiefly known for his operas.

WWW - World Wide Web.

ALSO BY IGOR NIKOLIC

The Space Legacy Series:

1. **The Spaceship In The Stone** (Book 1) Amazon & Audible
2. **Max's Logs Vol. 1** (Book 1.5) Amazon & Audible
3. **Orbital Ascension** (Book 2) Amazon & Audible
4. **Max's Logs Vol. 2** (Book 2.5) Amazon
5. **Ancient Enemies** (Book 3) Amazon
6. Max's Logs Vol. 3 (Book 3.5) - **TBP**
7. Solar Incursion (Book 4) - **TBP**
8. Max's Logs Vol. 4 (Book 4.5) - **TBP**

Adam Novus Chronicles Series:

1. The Death Curse (Book 1) - **TBP**
2. Tales Of The Hidden 1 (Book 1.5) - **TBP**
3. To Rule In Hell (Book 2) - **TBP**

***TBP** - **T**o **B**e Published

Printed in Great Britain
by Amazon